"*Adam!*" Haley Gasped,

thoroughly unnerved by his firm touch. "What are you doing?"

"Research," Adam murmured throatily.

"Like heck you are!" Everything had changed between them. Was it her fault? Or was it Adam's? Perhaps it was the fault of the romance book they were writing. She'd always been one to throw herself into her work heart and soul, but writing a romance was obviously not the same as writing a how-to book on plumbing or carpentry. Was this all a mistake?

Another kiss, Haley mused. She needed another kiss to help her decide.

LAURIEN BLAIR

writes, "I am having a great time writing romances because they are one of the few places where you can construct a perfect world, and the ending is always happy. The other thing I hope readers will find in my books is a sense of fun. My characters are going to laugh a lot, love a lot and have a great time, for in the end, that's really what I think falling in love is all about."

Dear Reader,

Thank you so much for all the letters I have received
praising our SILHOUETTE DESIRE series. All
your comments have proved invaluable to us, as we
strive to publish the best in contemporary romance.

DESIREs feature all of the elements you like to see
in a romance, plus a more sensual, provocative
story. So if you want to experience all the
excitement, passion and joy of falling in love,
then SILHOUETTE DESIRE is for you.

I hope you enjoy this book and all the wonderful
stories to come from SILHOUETTE DESIRE. If
you have any thoughts you'd like to share with us on
SILHOUETTE DESIRE, then please write to
me at the address below:

Jane Nicholls
Silhouette Books
PO Box 177
Dunton Green
Sevenoaks
Kent
TN13 2YE

LAURIEN BLAIR

Between The Covers

Silhouette *Desire*

Published by Silhouette Books

Copyright © 1984 by Laurien Blair

First printing 1984

British Library C.I.P.

Blair, Laurien
  Between the covers.—(Silhouette desire)
  I. Title
  813'.54[F]   PS3552.L346/

  ISBN 0 340 36165 4

Printed and bound in Great Britain for
Hodder and Stoughton Paperbacks, a
division of Hodder and Stoughton Ltd.,
Mill Road, Dunton Green, Sevenoaks,
Kent (Editorial Office: 47 Bedford
Square, London, WC1 3DP) by
Richard Clay (The Chaucer Press) Ltd.,
Bungay, Suffolk

Between
The Covers

1

"How does this sound?" Haley Morgan said thoughtfully. Propping her elbows on the kitchen table, she held up the sheet of paper, which was still rolled through her typewriter, and read what she had written, " 'The moment that she saw him, Allegra knew he was the one. Their eyes locked together in a heated gaze that drove all other thought from her mind.' "

As she read, Adam Burke leaned back in his chair at the other end of the table, lifting his long, khaki-clad legs to rest his feet on its thick glass top. The movement caught Haley's eye, and she glanced up, her gaze flickering over him briefly, noting the way the material of his blue knit polo shirt stretched tautly over the smooth muscles of his chest as he crossed his arms behind his head and closed his eyes to listen.

Then, frowning, she pulled her dark, tawny-brown eyes away and continued reading. " 'The people who milled around them in the crowded airport faded to insignificance. They might as well have been on a desert island, for they saw, they heard, they felt, only each other.' "

Finishing, she looked up expectantly. There was a brief moment of silence before Adam opened his eyes slowly and announced, "It sounds like a lot of baloney to me."

Glaring at him across the four-foot expanse of table, Haley ripped the sheet from the typewriter and tossed it aside in disgust. "I was afraid you'd say that," she groaned. "We're never going to be able to write this book. A romance, of all things! I don't know what's gotten into you to even suggest such a thing!"

Frowning, she rose from her chair, reaching up to rake her fingers through her long, silky black hair and push it back behind her shoulders, out of the way. "If you want my opinion, I think we ought to chuck this whole idea and do another self-help manual, just like we originally planned. *Cleaning Chimneys for Fun and Profit* is still doing great, and from all the advance interest we've had, it looks as though *Ten Easy Steps to Self-Actualization* may do even better. We've proven our ability in that area, and I think we should stick with it."

"That's exactly why now is the time for us to break loose and try something different," Adam pointed out, gazing up at her calmly. "With eight books in five years, we've already established ourselves as writers of nonfiction. What better time to try something new?"

"Easy for you to say—you're not the one who spent the whole morning trying to do nothing more than come up with an opening paragraph," Haley grumbled, but she smiled down at him reluctantly, already acknowledging, if not aloud, at least to herself, that Adam would probably be able to talk her around to looking at things his way, as he so often did.

Talk about stubborn! she thought. When Adam got hooked on an idea, he had a one-track mind. Not that he wasn't very often right, just that sometimes she had to try and moderate his enthusiasm. But then, after all this time, playing the voice of reason, Sancho Panza to his Don Quixote, was second nature to her now. Perhaps it was their differences that made them work so well as a team, she reflected, for it certainly was not what they had in common.

Adam, for his part, was wonderfully creative, his active imagination tending to spin off in all sorts of crazy directions, often spewing out ideas faster than he could write them down. He was a dreamer, an inventor, and an incurable optimist. She, on the other hand, lived by thinking and doing. She had a keen intellect, a knack for solving problems and a strong streak of practicality. Her mind was sharp and analytical, and she approached life with a cool, detached logic, at which Adam could only shake his head in wonder. The five years their partnership had lasted thus far had been a time of harmony and much success, as they discovered that their contradictory styles complemented one another beautifully, resulting in an impressive string of books whose topics ranged from weight lifting to macramé.

"Actually," said Adam, "you were the one who told me that romances were the hottest-selling books around at the moment. I thought you were all for the idea."

"That was before you told me that I'd be responsible for most of the writing, since we wanted to portray the woman's point of view!"

"I don't see what's wrong with that." Adam shrugged. "It sounds like a fair division of labor to me. I come up with the characters and the plot, and all you have to do is fill in the words."

"That's *all?*" Haley yelped in outrage before realizing that he was grinning at her broadly. Reaching down, she snatched up the discarded paper and wadded it quickly into a ball, then fired it at him point-blank. She watched with satisfaction as the paper hit him squarely between the eyes and bounced harmlessly away.

"That," she declared smugly, "is what I think of your romance!"

"Tsk tsk." Adam shook his head calmly, used to such displays of pique. "One day that temper of yours is going to get you into trouble."

"So what else is new?" Haley shrugged. Leaning down, she whisked the paper up off the floor and dropped it neatly into the full wastebasket that sat beside her chair. "Come on, we've been at this for hours. What do you say we break for lunch?"

They ate on Haley's back terrace, overlooking Long Island

Sound, one of the many features that had endeared the small cottage to her the moment she had first seen it six years earlier. The guest house of a large estate in the Belle Haven section of Greenwich, Connecticut, it was situated on the back edge of the owner's property, where skillful landscaping ensured both his privacy and her own. Though small, it was bright and cheerful and airy, an effect achieved in part by her careful choice of furnishings. Light wood and wicker predominated, glass-top tables were scattered throughout, and the couch, the curtains and all the pillows were done in Laura Ashley fabrics in pastel shades of pink and blue.

Summers, they did all their writing there; the windows and doors were thrown open to catch the breeze that came in off the Sound, cooling them as they hunched over their matching Smith-Coronas, placed on either end of the table in the tiny dining alcove. Like birds, they migrated in winter, packing up their gear and moving their communal office several miles north to Adam's cozy condominium in back-country Greenwich. There they made ample use of the large fireplace, burning several cords of woods each year as they sprawled in front of its cheery warmth, their portable typewriters resting once more back to back on opposite ends of the coffee table. Five days a week, they lived in each other's pockets, a relationship that by all rights should have driven them crazy; instead, their association had thrived, and their friendship deepened and flourished.

Adam made the pitcher of iced tea while Haley slapped together several tuna sandwiches on rye. Setting the offering down on the picnic table, she poured herself a glass of tea, then settled back on one of the lounge chairs, her slim, tanned legs stretched out before her on the long cushion.

In repose, her features lost their animation, but not their arresting quality. Haley's face, with its classic bones, wide almond-shaped eyes and honey-toned skin, was the sort that would always draw a second glance, and then perhaps a third. Her hair, a lustrous, flowing black mane, lay fanned out on the pillow behind her. She stretched luxuriously, basking in the warm golden touch of the sun's rays. Dressed in a pair of short, faded cutoffs and a skimpy red tank top, she had chosen her clothes with the balmy June weather in mind, and now they provided scarcely more coverage than a bathing suit, no deterrent at all to the glowing tan she was cultivating.

"You know you shouldn't get so much sun," Adam said conversationally from his seat across the terrace, in the shade. "You'll get old before your time, dry up like a prune. Do you realize that I'm sitting here right now watching your skin turn to leather?"

"Shhh!" Haley muttered, not bothering to open her eyes.

Adam had never been able to understand her love affair with the sun. As far as he was concerned, it was meant to be taken in small doses, and then only if one was liberally slathered with lotion. Waving her hand in his general direction, she dismissed his advice as carelessly as one might brush away a pesky fly. "Don't bother me. I'm thinking."

"Sure you are," Adam agreed, reaching for his second sandwich. "And I'm Norman Mailer. Between the two of us, we ought to have this book written in no time."

"If you want to stem the tide of creative genius . . ." Haley let her voice trail away meaningfully. Adam's only answer to that was a barely discernible grunt, and her lips curved upward in a small, satisfied smile. That shut him up! No doubt he thought she was mapping out another opening paragraph to replace the one he'd panned earlier, and perhaps in time she would. But for now, the sun felt deliciously warm and relaxing, and she had no desire to work at all.

Reclining against the flowered cushion, Haley let her thoughts wander, knowing from experience that the best ideas often occurred to her when she wasn't actively involved in seeking them out. This time, however, the plan went somewhat awry. Instead of solving the problem of the unwritten romance, she found herself drifting back in time, remembering, with a writer's capacity for detail, the day that she and Adam had first met, seven years earlier.

She'd been in college in Boston then and was home on spring break, spending two weeks with her family at their Manhattan apartment before returning to the grueling battery of final exams that would finish off her junior year. On her first day home, she'd spent the afternoon at a nearby health club, enjoying a game of pickup racket ball, then a dip in the pool, then meeting some friends in the coffee shop for an early dinner of salad and quiche. By the time she'd made her way home, it was almost eight o'clock. Letting herself into her parent's Park Avenue co-op, Haley had thrown down her gear in the front hall, picked up the mail from the table and was thumbing through it idly as she wandered into the living room.

"Anybody home?" she called out without looking up as she flipped through a colorful Bloomingdale's catalogue.

"Yes, actually," said a deep voice that sounded startlingly near, and Haley raised her eyes just in time to take in the sight of a charcoal-gray jacket and blue silk tie at very close range before her momentum sent her crashing into a rather large obstacle that hadn't bothered to move from her path.

"Oh!" she gasped, utterly startled, as the mail slipped from her fingers and cascaded to the floor.

Immediately, his hands reached out to grasp her shoulders lightly, steadying her as she stepped back and righted herself, an apology forming on her lips. The words were never spoken, however, for as Haley looked up, she found herself gazing into a pair of eyes that were quite the most compelling shade of silver gray she had ever seen. Automatically then, her gaze swept over him, noting with approval that the rest of the package wasn't half bad, either.

He was taller than she was, but not too tall, his body trim and muscular beneath the stylish cut of his Italian suit. His hair was a deep, rich mahogany brown, and it had been brushed back negligently off a face that was characterized by high, jutting cheekbones and a strong, determined jaw. His mouth was wide, his lips full and sensual, and already small creases were beginning to form on either side, attesting to the fact that he smiled easily, as indeed he was doing now—grinning, actually, Haley decided, in a wonderfully disarming way, with all the pleased self-assurance of a man who knows who he is and where he's going.

"Good evening," he said pleasantly, dropping his hands from her shoulders and then, in the same motion, bending down to gather up the mail, which lay scattered about their feet.

Above him, Haley could only stand and stare, suddenly conscious that her hair was gathered into two long braids on either side of her head, her face was bare of makeup, and the slouchy, elbow-patched sweater she wore had once belonged to her father.

"Who are you?" she demanded without stopping to think, her resentment at being caught out by such a gorgeous hunk of manhood giving the question a much sharper tone than she'd intended.

"Adam Burke," the hunk supplied, gray eyes twinkling merrily. He stood back up and delivered the mail into her outstretched hand. "At your service."

Well, that didn't tell her anything, Haley thought, quickly turning the name over in her mind. Perhaps he was an associate of her father's; he certainly had the presence to be a courtroom attorney. Or maybe he was a client, falsely accused of his crime, of course.

"You must be Haley," Adam continued. "Helen talks about you often."

"Helen?" she echoed blankly, so caught up in her fantasy of him as a maligned victim of the city's circuitous judicial process that for a moment she was quite unable to grasp the truth.

"Your sister," Adam prompted. Then, when no response was forthcoming, he said lightly, "At least I hope you have a sister named Helen. Otherwise, I'm afraid I've come to the wrong apartment."

"Oh!" Haley sputtered, hastily realigning her thoughts. "Yes, of course." Good God, this man was her sister's date! She should have thought of that right off, but she'd been so dazzled

13

that it hadn't occurred to her at all, and now he probably thought she was not only clumsy but a moron as well! Quickly, she strove to recover her composure. "Has someone gone to let her know you're here?"

Adam nodded. "Your father's doing that now."

"Well, then," said Haley, covering her confusion by stepping into the role of hostess, "would you like something to drink while you wait?"

Without waiting for his reply, she started toward the bar in the corner of the room, only to be brought up short by the cool amusement in his tone as he said, "Surely you aren't planning to fix it yourself? I'm afraid I've gone a bit beyond the Shirley Temple stage."

Shirley Temple indeed! Haley fumed silently. Just how old did he think she was, anyway?

"Don't worry," she retorted. "I know how to make the grown-up drinks, too. Or maybe," she added, looking back over her shoulder coolly, "you'd rather that I just tossed you a can of beer so that you can rip off the top and drink it he-man style?"

"So the kid has claws," Adam murmured appreciatively.

At that, Haley whirled in her tracks and planted her hands atop her hips, quivering with indignation. "I'm not a kid!" she announced in defense of her twenty years, knowing even as she did so that it was hard to look mature when you stood five feet two, weighed barely one hundred pounds wet and had two long braids hanging halfway down your back.

"Pardon me. The *lady* has claws," Adam amended smoothly, but his quick, slashing grin negated any gains Haley might have felt she had made.

"Woman," she snapped, correcting him irritably.

"Oh, no!" Adam cried in mock horror. "A feminist!"

"Actually," Haley said silkily, "I prefer the term humanist. It implies a much more broadly based concept."

An expression of surprise flickered briefly across his face, then was gone, Adam obviously having reassessed his earlier evaluation. "If we're going to argue semantics," he informed her with a smile, "then I feel I must warn you that, as a writer, I'm on intimate terms with my thesaurus."

Abruptly, Haley grinned. "Whatever turns you on . . ." she retorted, her brown eyes glinting wickedly.

The reply that Adam was about to make was cut off, however, for her parents chose that moment to return to the living room, followed closely behind by Helen, her older sister. Instead, his eyes found hers, and he inclined his head slightly in silent recognition of her worthiness as an opponent in their verbal byplay. Then, in a movement so unexpected that Haley wondered later if she might have imagined it, he dropped one eyelid in a quick conspiratorial wink before turning away to shake hands with her mother and greet her sister warmly.

Over the next two weeks, Haley found out quite a lot about Mr. Adam Burke, for her sister spoke of him constantly. Beautiful, magnetic Helen, who flitted from man to man with all the fickle constancy of a butterfly skimming from bloom to bloom, though for the brief period each shared her favor, she was utterly absorbed, always sure that this time she had found true love. Through her, Haley discovered that Adam lived in nearby Connecticut, possessed a degree in journalism from Columbia and worked as a reporter for a New York daily newspaper. To someone of her limited experience, he seemed utterly sophisticated and totally fascinating, the six-year difference in their ages only serving to enhance the immediate attraction she had felt.

All of which Haley very carefully and conscientiously squelched. She adored her older sister, after all; but beyond that there was a matter of principles—she was not the man-stealing type and never would be. No, she knew very clearly right from the start, that Adam Burke was very definitely off limits.

That, however, didn't stop them from running into one another at odd moments. On those evenings when he came to pick up Helen, they would often chat for several minutes while her sister finished dressing, Adam still teasingly referring to her as "the kid," a nickname Haley finally accepted with grudging good will, deciding that under the circumstances, it was probably just as well. The following July, he'd been invited to spend a week with her family at their house in Southampton, a time that Haley remembered as a succession of long, lazy days on the beach, all of them together swimming and sunning, and through it all, she and Adam talking endlessly.

"Are you sure you don't mind?" Haley had inquired anxiously, slipping into her sister's room late one night for a chat, a habit that dated back to their childhood years.

"Not at all," Helen reassured her, reclining back onto the banked pillows of her bed with a lazy yawn. "Actually, I'm sort of glad the two of you get along so well. It saves me the trouble of having to be witty and entertaining all the time. Besides, you've always been the brainy one in the family, so how could I mind that? Adam and I have—" She paused and smiled discreetly, "other things in common."

By the time Adam and Helen's romance fizzled at the end of the summer, he and Haley had already built a friendship that seemed destined to do better. Several times during her senior year at college, when his work had brought him up to Boston, they had met for coffee and a pizza, falling quickly back into the easy camaraderie that had come to characterize their relationship. When, upon graduation, Haley decided that she'd had enough of city life, it was Adam who suggested that she look for a place in his home town of Greenwich, a community that embodied the quiet country charm of Connecticut, while remaining an easy commute from downtown Manhattan. In short order, Haley had managed to secure the guest house and then, less than a month later, a job as well, when she was taken on in an entry-level position at a large New York ad agency.

For a time, it seemed as though she had everything—a good job with plenty of potential, a great house and several close friends, including Adam, whom she had come to depend on as a trusted confidante. Her boss was one of the agency's rising stars, an ambitious young account executive with dashing good looks and an easy brand of charm, and when he began singling her out for special attention, Haley felt she was on top of the world. Their relationship quickly progressed from nights spent working late together at the office to intimate dinners for two at some of New York's finest restaurants. Enthralled as she was by his constant flattery and attention, Haley threw herself into her work, lavishing his pet projects with time and devotion. They would go far together, he told her, and she believed him.

Later, she would realize that it was a measure of her naïveté about how the business world was run that months had passed before she discovered, quite by accident, that all the credit for the ad campaigns whose ideas she had developed and nurtured so lovingly was reflecting back on only one person, and it wasn't she. Fired by indignation, she'd confronted her boss with this new-found knowledge, only to be delivered a cool, deliberate ultimatum. Either put up with the situation, or get out. Haley left the very same day, almost a full year's worth of work down the drain, with nothing to show for it but the lesson she had learned the hard way. Business and pleasure were two areas that simply did not mix. It was a mistake she did not intend to make again.

It had seemed entirely natural for her to pour out her troubles on Adam's shoulder—only six months earlier she had listened while he debated his growing disenchantment with journalism and his desire to strike out on his own. The book proposal she'd encouraged him to write had already found a publisher. The manuscript, however, lay languishing, less than half complete, while Adam found himself bogged down in seemingly endless research. As her bills continued to mount alarmingly and no solid job prospects appeared on the horizon, they drifted toward one another naturally, finally realizing that for them to join forces, with Haley in the position of research assistant, was the solution to both their problems.

Just when she had stopped being Adam's assistant and started being his partner wasn't exactly clear, but in her new job, Haley discovered an aptitude for writing that she'd never even suspected. She threw herself into the project wholeheartedly, her dedication so complete that in the end, her contribution to the final manuscript nearly equaled Adam's own, a fact that he had the good grace to concede. To Haley's delight, he'd had the book contract amended, naming her as coauthor, and the team of Burke and Morgan, self-help experts, was born.

In the previous five years, their partnership had prospered and their friendship solidified. The channels of communication were wide open between them in all areas but one. To that day, their relationship remained totally platonic. There had been times in the past, years earlier, when Haley had hoped that that might change. Back in her college days and even after, Adam had been the subject of countless romantic fantasies, as she nurtured the hope that he would someday come to see her as something more than "the kid."

It had been some time since he'd called her that, Haley realized suddenly. Not that it really mattered anymore, for now their lives were inextricably bound together in far too many other ways. Their reliance on one another now extended into the professional sphere as well. Adam was not only her best friend but also the source of her livelihood, and she had come a long way from the starry-eyed romantic child she'd once been. Far enough to be much too practical to jeopardize what they had by chasing the elusive fulfillment that change might or might not bring. No, Haley decided, she was quite content with things just the way they were.

"Come on, lazybones," said Adam, prodding her shoulder none too gently and bringing her out of her reverie with a start. "Time to get back to work."

Looking up in surprise, Haley blinked rapidly several times to bring her eyes back into focus and found that he was standing just behind the chaise, towering over her and grinning with amusement.

"No sleeping on the job around here!" he announced, nudging her shoulder once more. "Come on, up you go!"

"I wasn't sleeping," Haley defended herself. She climbed reluctantly up off the lounger and stretched. "I was thinking."

"So you mentioned before," said Adam, his tone clearly conveying his disbelief. "If that's so, then I'm sure by now you must have come up with the perfect opening paragraph for *Passionate Strangers*."

"*Passionate Strangers* indeed," Haley grumbled, picking up the dishes on the table and following him inside to dump them into the sink. "Where did you ever come up with that title, anyway?"

"What's the matter with it?" Adam asked, pretending to take offense. "I happen to think it's great. It has everything— excitement, mystery, erotic suspense. Besides, the least you could do is humor me. After all, did I complain when you named our carpentry book *Love Yourself, Love Your House?*"

"It sold, didn't it?" Haley retorted, smiling at the recollection, "and I still think it was the perfect name for a book on the Gestalt theory of carpentry."

"Just as *Passionate Strangers* is the perfect name for our romance," Adam continued smoothly. "What else would you call a book where the hero and heroine meet each other totally by chance on the first page and fall madly in love shortly thereafter?"

"I see what you mean," said Haley, frowning thoughtfully. "Is that really what the tip sheet said?"

"See for yourself," Adam invited, taking up his seat at one end of the table. He thumbed quickly through the scattered papers that lay between them, found what he was after and sent it sailing down the table top.

Silently, Haley read through the list of requirements. "All right," she said finally, resigning herself to her fate. "I guess if this is what you really want, then *Passionate Strangers* it is. But next time," she added sternly, jabbing her finger at him for emphasis, "it will be my turn to choose the subject *and* the title."

"Done," Adam agreed quickly, and Haley knew he was

savoring the victory enormously but, to his credit, trying hard not to show it. "Now, madam collaborator, if you don't mind, can we get started?"

"Of course," Haley demurred. Taking out a fresh sheet of white paper, she rolled it through her typewriter, then sat, her fingers poised just above the keys. "Anytime you're ready," she said sweetly.

Across the table, Adam frowned. "What about all that thinking you were doing outside?"

Haley's shrug was slow and eloquent.

"That's what I was afraid of," Adam groaned, leaning back in his chair. "All right, give me a moment."

Five minutes passed, and then ten. Glaring down at the blank sheet of paper before her, Haley began to drum her fingers on the glass table top impatiently as each waited in silence for inspiration to strike.

"I've got it!" she cried suddenly, and Adam glanced up in pleased surprise.

"The opening paragraph?" he asked hopefully.

"No," Haley admitted, and watched his face fall, "the reason why we can't seem to get started. Maybe the problem is that we've never tried to deal with characters before and we don't know ours well enough. Rather than trying to jump right in and write a scene, why don't we begin by doing a quick character sketch first?"

"Good idea," Adam said, nodding his approval.

"Think for a moment," said Haley, resting her elbow on the table and cupping her chin in her hand. "Then describe Allegra to me, exactly as you imagine her."

"Let me see," Adam said slowly, picturing the heroine in his mind's eye. "Well, for starters, she has to be a blonde—say, about five foot six, with long, long legs. And of course," he added almost as an afterthought, "she'd have to be very well built."

"Of course," Haley agreed solemnly.

Across the tops of the two typewriters, Adam gazed at her suspiciously. "What's the matter with that?" he demanded.

"Nothing," Haley shrugged, her eyebrows raised in innocence. "She sounds perfect."

"Good," Adam said firmly, reaching for a piece of typing paper to put into his machine.

"After all," Haley mused aloud, "that is the traditional profile of the all-American beauty."

Glancing up from what he was doing, Adam's gray eyes narrowed fractionally. "Beautiful women come in all shapes and sizes," he said. "All I did was pick one that I thought would appeal to a broad spectrum of readers."

"She'll do that, all right," Haley agreed, finding herself quite fascinated by his description of the ideal heroine. Unwittingly, her eyes were drawn downward over her own figure, and without realizing it, she sighed aloud.

Not that there was really anything wrong with the way she looked, Haley admitted. It wasn't that she was unaware of her own appeal, rather that she was indifferent to it, her lush, dark, unusual brand of beauty having nothing in common with the fragile, feminine, porcelain looks that she herself considered ideal. Yet men had always seemed to find her attractive, and she supposed that ought to count for something. But still . . .

"Something the matter?" asked Adam, breaking into her thoughts.

With a quick, self-conscious smile, Haley shook her head. "Just wishful thinking, that's all." As always, she had no qualms at all about telling him what was on her mind. "Allegra sounds like something else. I wouldn't mind looking like that myself."

Finishing with the sheet of paper, Adam gave her his full attention. "Really?" he said, cocking one eyebrow curiously, "What's wrong with the way you look now?"

"For openers," Haley said bluntly, "I'm short."

"Not short," Adam corrected her with a grin. "Petite."

"I'm too skinny."

"Slender," he countered quickly, the amused expression on his face daring her to continue.

Looking downward disparagingly, Haley knew she had him now. "I'm flat as a board."

At that, Adam laughed out loud. Then slowly, deliberately, he let his eyes follow the same path hers had taken, and Haley felt herself growing uncomfortably warm beneath the careful scrutiny of his hooded gaze. What in the world was going on here? she wondered with no small measure of dismay. What was Adam doing? Why, in all the time they'd known each other, he'd never looked at her like *that* before. They'd only been kidding around, hadn't they? She'd meant to provoke his laughter, not this unexpected and thoroughly unnerving appraisal.

"I don't see anything wrong with your figure," Adam said finally when he'd raised his eyes once more. "Didn't anyone ever tell you that it's proportion, not size, that makes the difference?"

"That's easy for you to say," Haley bantered back quickly, relieved to have their communication restored to verbal channels once more. "You're not the one who looks like some of your best parts got left on the assembly line."

Still grinning, Adam shrugged. "Look on the bright side. Think of all the money you save by not having to buy bras."

"Thanks a lot," Haley sniffed.

"Not only that," Adam continued, obviously undaunted, "but you'll never have to worry about sagging like most women do."

"Terrific," Haley groaned, shaking her head. "That's just the sort of cheery thought that will keep me warm on a cold winter's night."

"Don't knock it. You'll be glad when you're sixty."

"I'll try to remember that," Haley shot back, "but in the meantime, do you know how nice it would be to just once really fill out a bathing suit? To walk past a construction sight and hear wolf whistles? To hold a conversation with a man who couldn't quite manage to keep his eyes on your face?"

"No," Adam admitted, answering her rhetorical questions, "quite frankly, I don't."

"You wouldn't," Haley snapped, suddenly losing her temper, although she wasn't quite sure why.

Gazing over at her, Adam frowned. "Are you feeling all right?" he asked solicitously. "You've been awfully touchy all day. I've never seen a book have this effect on you before."

"That's because you've never insisted on writing a romance before!" Haley growled, then immediately felt contrite. It wasn't Adam's fault that she wasn't in love with his latest brainchild. And she had promised to give it a try, so why was it that she felt herself rebelling at every turn? "I don't know, Adam. I just can't seem to get the hang of this. Everything we've done before has been strictly realistic, and yet romances like the one you want to write about never seem to happen in real life. At least I know I've never seen one."

"Sure they do," Adam replied. "You just haven't found yours yet, but it will come. Look at Prince Charles and Lady Diana, Edward VIII and Wallis Simpson . . ."

"Maybe I should try moving to England," Haley muttered facetiously under her breath.

"Mark Antony and Cleopatra . . ."

"I don't care what you say. I'm not moving to Egypt!"

"I should hope not," said Adam. "What good would you be to me on the other side of the world when your typewriter is sitting right here?"

"Work, work, work," Haley grumbled good-naturedly. Somehow Adam had the uncanny knack of always being able to make her smile. "Is that all you ever think about?"

"Ah, my spirited beauty," Adam cried, grinning at her lecherously as he twirled an imaginary moustache, "wouldn't you like to know?"

"Maybe I'll ask Sheila," Haley threatened teasingly, naming

his current girl friend. "She and I could have a little chat. You know, girl talk?"

"That's all I need," Adam groaned. "Can't a man have any secrets?"

"Do you mean after all these years there are still things about you I don't know?" Haley inquired sweetly. "Or are you more afraid that I might spill the beans to Sheila and let her know what a slave driver you really are?"

Feigning a lack of concern, Adam shrugged. "Sheila already knows all about my little perversions."

"Perversions!" Haley yelped. "This is even better than I suspected—you mean like whips and leather and wild animals . . . ?"

"Ha-ley!" Adam intoned warningly.

"No, wait!" she cried suddenly, the idea coming to her in a flash as ideas always did. "Adam, I've got it. This is perfect!" Pulling her chair in closer to the table, she began to type furiously. "We'll take Allegra and Rex out of the airport and put them in the jungle! You're going to love it! Let me tell you how it's going to go . . ."

2

I really think he's gone off the deep end this time," Haley declared as she opened the cardboard box on the counter and slid another slice of mushroom pizza onto her plate. "First, for wanting to write a romance at all, and now, for getting so excited about the idea that he's got us working practically day and night to get it done."

It was Friday night, and she was seated in the home of her good friend T. J. McFarland, a warm, outgoing woman with a headful of pixyish sandy-blonde curls, sparkling blue eyes and a wide mouth with a ready smile. They had met several years earlier at the information desk of the Greenwich library and had liked one another on sight. A friendship fostered by mutual interests and an unfailing delight in each other's company had quickly developed, and when T. J. had called earlier to say that her husband, Dan, was going out to a bachelor party while she remained home with baby Jeremy, Haley had obliged by inviting herself over to dinner.

The pizza had been her contribution to the meal, and T. J. had supplied the beer. They'd already polished off one apiece, and now Haley waited, tilting her stool back precariously on two legs, while her friend opened the refrigerator and pulled out two more bottles. "I swear I don't know what's gotten into him," she added as T. J. set the drinks down on the high counter that served as a divider between the living room and the kitchen, then sat down across from her on the other stool.

"So the man's a fanatic about his writing." T. J. shrugged dismissively. "He always has been; you know that. The two of you are so different from one another that it's ridiculous. How you ever manage to work together at all has always had me baffled. This is what, your ninth book?" She paused for a bite of pizza, fitting the long wedge carefully into her mouth as Haley nodded. "And every time you start a new project, it's the same story. Adam throws himself into the thing head over heels because all he can think about is the amount of work that needs to be done to finish the book, while for the very same reason, you hang back, sure that this time the topic you've picked is too tough and you're never going to be able to do it. Think back to your other books—getting started has always been rough. The problem is that you and Adam are both nervous. You just have different ways of showing it, that's all."

"Do you really think so?" Haley asked, frowning slightly.

"I'd bet my Ph.D. in clinical psychology on it."

"You don't have a Ph.D. in clinical psychology," Haley pointed out pleasantly. She reached for a bottle of beer and twisted off its cap.

"All right, then," T. J. conceded easily. "My M.A. in library science."

"Close enough, I suppose." Haley laughed. "Thank you for your analysis, Dr. McFarland."

"Anytime," T. J. said modestly. "After all, that's what I'm here for, solving the problems of the world."

"Aside from being a wife and mother and head librarian of the town library, you mean?"

"Mere diversions," T. J. sniffed. "They keep me off the streets. But the other calling . . ." The women looked at each other and dissolved in helpless laughter.

"Well, I'll say one thing for you," Haley admitted. "You do have a way of keeping me from taking myself too seriously."

"Good." T. J. nodded. "Now that that's settled, I want to

hear all about the book. I must admit I'm finding this rather fascinating, it being your first work of fiction and all. How's it going?"

"Not bad at all," said Haley. Lifting the box cover once more, she surveyed the two remaining pieces, then settled for picking the mushrooms and cheese off the nearest one. "We've done the first two chapters, and so far Allegra and her intrepid hero Rex seem to be sorting themselves out pretty well."

"Hey, cut that out!" T. J. scolded, seeing what she was doing and slapping her hand away. "No fair just eating the good parts!"

Across the counter, Haley grinned unrepentantly as she tore off the whole slice and hoisted it onto her plate. "There," she griped, "are you satisfied now?"

Primly, T. J. nodded. Then her eyes widened as Haley began picking the pizza apart once more, this time from the privacy of her own plate. Shaking her head, she let an indelicate snort serve as her only comment on the proceedings.

"It's still going pretty slowly, though," said Haley, popping a mushroom into her mouth. "You know Adam. He thinks research is the most important thing in the world. Now he's looking into boats." Dramatically, she rolled her eyes heavenward.

"Boats?" T. J. echoed. "What do they have to do with romance?"

"In my book, nothing," Haley said firmly, "but I think Adam has some sort of a crazy idea about a romantic interlude on the high seas. Apparently, the native craft in the area where we've dropped them is something called a catamaran, and now Adam's trying to borrow one so we can learn how to sail."

"Mmm," said T. J., savoring the last bite of pizza, "that sounds like fun."

"Fun?" Haley cried. "I think it sounds awful. I hate boats! When I was little, my parents took us on a cruise, and I've never yet been able to live down the fact that I got seasick on the *Queen Elizabeth*."

"Don't worry about it," said T. J., licking off each of her fingers in turn. "On small boats, it's different. You're out in the fresh air, not down in some stuffy cabin."

"If you like the idea so much, why don't you go in my place?" Haley proposed. "I'd be happy to watch Jeremy for you. You can take notes and tell me all about it when you get back."

"Oh, no, you don't." T. J. shook her head. "You're not roping me into doing your work for you. Besides, if you end up on the bounding main, you'll have only yourself to blame. After all, who was it who took those two poor, unsuspecting characters and dropped them down in the wilds of Samoa, anyway?"

"It did seem like such a good idea at the time." Haley sighed.

"You'll figure something out," T. J. assured her blithely. Reaching over, she flipped the top of the pizza box shut, piled their two plates on top of it, then pushed the whole thing aside. "Now," she said, "that's enough shop talk for one evening. Time to get on to the good stuff. How's your love life doing these days?"

"Same as it was last time you asked," Haley replied, her voice deliberately bland. She was used to dealing with her friend's outspoken curiosity. "On a scale of one to ten—"

"On a scale of one to ten, with your record, you'd barely make the chart!" T. J. hooted. "All I can say is it's a good thing you're not my only single friend, because if I had to rely on you for all my vicarious thrills, I'd be in sorry shape indeed!"

"Hey, come on, I'm not doing *that* badly," Haley protested laughingly.

"Are you still seeing good old Cliff?"

Haley nodded, picturing the man to whom T. J. referred, a good-looking young lawyer she'd been dating sporadically for the past month.

T. J. thumped her hand on the counter for emphasis. "I rest my case!"

"Don't be silly," said Haley. "Cliff and I have a good time

together. Tomorrow night we're going out to that new French restaurant in Westport with Adam and Sheila."

"You're doubling with Adam and Sheila?" T. J. cried in delight, momentarily sidetracked. "Oh, to be a fly on the wall for that one!"

"What do you mean?" asked Haley, cocking one eyebrow upward. "I don't see anything wrong with that. Adam and I often double date with other people."

"But not these two." T. J. chortled. "Just wait until they get a load of one another. Cliff, the hypersmart, overeducated Harvard lawyer, and Sheila, the woman who is living proof of the theory of inverse proportion between IQ and bra size. Believe me, it should be quite an evening!"

In spite of herself, Haley had to laugh. She hadn't thought of it in quite that way before, but now that she did, she could see that T. J. was right. Cliff and Sheila were poles apart in almost every way.

"Really, Haley," T. J. said earnestly, not allowing herself to be put off for long, "as your friend, I know I should be the last person to criticize your taste in men, but as long as you keep seeing Cliff, I'm afraid I just can't help myself. I mean, I know he's good-looking and all, but don't you ever find him just the tiniest bit—well, dull?"

"Dull?" Haley echoed innocently, although she knew full well what T. J. was referring to.

Cliff was a member of one of Greenwich's fine old society families, and as such, his life had been programmed into the correct patterns since birth. He'd been to the right schools, chosen the right profession, even wore the right clothes, his moneyed upbringing resulting in a view of life that was as conservative and narrow-minded as it was predictable.

"Yes, dull," T. J. repeated forcibly. "You know, boring, right down to his wing-tip shoes. Honestly, Haley, that man is about as exciting as week-old bread. If you ask me, it's those old society genes of his—I think they've had all the spontaneity bred right out of them."

"So he isn't perfect," Haley allowed with a shrug. "Not many people are, you know."

"He's not the man for you; any dope could see that. What you really need," T. J. said wisely, "is a good love affair."

"Doesn't everybody?" Haley sighed. "But in case nobody ever told you, good men don't exactly grow on trees."

"How would you know?" T. J. scoffed. "You've hardly been out looking. Why, in the whole time I've known you, I've never seen you get really serious about anyone. You've got to loosen up, girl, go with the flow."

"The last time I went with the flow," Haley said cynically, "it carried me straight to the unemployment line, remember?"

"So you had one bad experience. So what? After all this time, don't you think you're about ready to climb back on the horse?"

Shaking her head, Haley laughed out loud at her friend's imagery. "Don't worry. I haven't given up on men entirely. It's just that, for now, I'm biding my time until the right one comes along."

"And when he does?" T. J. prompted.

"Then I shall act accordingly," Haley replied, her brown eyes dancing impishly. "I'll simply throw myself into his arms and demand to be carried off into the sunset."

"All right," T. J. conceded, finally backing down. "Just as long as you've got a game plan ready."

She stood up, gathered up the dishes and carried them over to the sink. "You know," she said, delivering one last parting shot back over her shoulder, "maybe writing this romance will turn out to be good for you—put you in the right frame of mind, so to speak."

"Maybe," Haley agreed, though her voice lacked conviction. Looking down, she checked the time on the tank watch on her wrist. "Speaking of writing, however, I'm afraid I'm going to have to make this an early night. I've got a million things to do tomorrow, and on top of everything else, Adam and I have gotten roped into doing a promotion for *How to Be Your Own Plumber's Helper.*"

"What kind of promotion?" T. J. opened up the dishwasher and began tossing plates inside with a display of reckless abandon that Haley couldn't help but admire.

"You know the sort of thing," she said, sliding down off her stool and walking around the counter into the kitchen to help. " 'Local pair makes good' and all that. We're going to spend tomorrow morning autographing books in a hardware store, of all places, and we've got to be in Stamford by nine."

Lifting the door to the dishwasher with her toe, T. J. caught it with her knee and nudged it shut. "I thought writers were supposed to autograph books in nice clean book stores," she commented as she wiped her hands dry on the seat of her pants.

"So did I." Haley shrugged helplessly. "But the publicity department wanted to try something different. They've decided that we're going to go where the market is rather than letting it come to us. You don't suppose if we did a book about gambling in European casinos the publishers might be convinced to . . ." She let her voice trail away hopefully, noting even as she did so that T. J. was already shaking her head. "No? I didn't think so, either."

Several minutes later, after stopping to look in on Jeremy, T. J. walked Haley to the door. "You know," she said thoughtfully, "it seems like forever since the four of us have gotten together to play bridge. I know you and Adam have been extra busy lately—"

"Not to mention the way Jeremy seems to cut into your free time," Haley interjected teasingly.

"So maybe all our lives have gotten a little crowded since we used to make a regular Wednesday night thing of it," T. J. admitted. "Still, I'll talk to Dan, and why don't you see if you can nail down Adam. Maybe we can set something up for next week?"

"You're on, if I can manage it," Haley promised, and meant it. She'd sorely missed their hard-fought matches—all four of them being good, solid, aggressive players who bid and played to win. "I'll give you a call early in the week, and we'll pick a day."

The next morning, Adam arrived at the cottage at quarter past eight, a full fifteen minutes earlier than she'd expected him, and Haley, as usual, was running late. At the sound of his knock, she swore inelegantly under her breath, hands poised above her head as she quickly unwound the last of the electric curlers from her hair. Adam hated it when she was late; she knew that. In fact, it annoyed him almost as much as his habit of always being early irritated her.

"Come on in," she called, her voice severely hampered by the mouthful of hairpins she held carefully between her lips. "I'll be right out."

Spitting the pins out onto her dresser, Haley's fingers flew over the buttons of her brown silk blouse before jamming it down inside the waistband of her skirt. At least this time there was a good reason for her tardiness, she justified to herself, for she'd certainly *started* getting ready early enough. What she hadn't counted on was wasting the better part of an hour trying to decide what to wear. After all, how was she supposed to know what was proper attire for a hardware store?

Actually, her first impulse had been to emulate Josephine the Plumber—to go with her face scrubbed clean, her hair tucked up underneath a baseball cap and wearing an old pair of overalls in the hope that her looks might impart an aura of credibility to her work. That idea was quickly discarded, however, when Haley realized that she didn't own a pair of overalls and never had. Besides, she'd decided, denying her femininity wasn't going to gain her anything in the long run. No, the only sensible thing to do was to aim for a look that was poised, confident and, above all, professional.

With that in mind, she had chosen a tailored outfit. A sleek cream-colored linen suit that flattered her body without flaunting it was worn over a demure bow-tie blouse in a rich shade of taupe. The idea of curling her hair had been a last-minute impulse. It wasn't something she did often, and viewing the frizzy results in the mirror over her dresser, Haley was inclined to wish that she hadn't thought of doing it.

Brushing away furiously in an attempt to tame the curls into some semblance of order, she slipped one foot into its sling-back pump and was nosing around on the floor with her toe for the other when she heard the front door open and shut, signaling that Adam had let himself in.

"Haley!"

The tone of voice alone was a bit of an attention grabber, but add to that the effect of its unexpected nearness, and Haley jumped straight up in the air, dropping the hairbrush, which hit the dresser with a loud clatter, then rolled down onto the floor. She turned to find Adam standing in the bedroom doorway.

"Aren't you ready yet?" He frowned, taking in her somewhat disheveled appearance.

"Do I look ready?" Haley demanded, blowing a small stream of air upward at the wayward curls that hung down over her eyes and obscured her vision. Balancing precariously on one foot, she strove to marshal her dignity.

Glaring at him crossly, she noted that if Adam had been plagued by the same sartorial doubts as she had, neither his arrival time nor his appearance reflected it. His outfit—a pair of crisp white cotton twill pants, a yellow open-neck polo shirt and a well-cut navy blazer—was casual, yet worn with an air of self-confidence and quiet authority, which immediately stamped him as a man to be taken seriously.

"Actually," Adam commented, his gray eyes glittering with amusement, "you look like the victim of a freak tornado."

"Thanks a lot," Haley muttered as she clomped, one foot up, one foot down, across the room and brushed past him on her way to the kitchen. Perhaps if she poured him a cup of coffee, he'd be less inclined to notice the passage of time. And maybe, she added to herself wryly, with something in his mouth, he'd be less able to complain.

Glancing back over her shoulder, she couldn't resist adding, "I would have thought that a man of your vast experience would already know that most women don't look perfect first thing in the morning."

"They may not look perfect," said Adam, squinting down at her playfully as he followed her into the kitchen, "but they usually don't look *that* bad."

Reaching the counter, Haley whirled in her tracks, no mean feat considering the state of her footwear, and found that Adam was right behind her. The retort she was about to make died on her lips, however, as he surprised her by reaching out and tangling his fingers through her thick, dark hair, lifting the heavy curls back off her face. "What in the world have you done to your hair, anyway?"

With a thoroughly unexpected shock of awareness, Haley felt the hair on the back of her neck begin to tingle, awakened by the delicate, caressing touch of his hand. "I curled it," she said, stating the obvious with a small toss of her head that was part defensive maneuver and partly a shiver of reaction. "What's the matter? Don't you like it?"

"I hate it," Adam growled. Ignoring her defiant gesture, he moved his hand slightly so that the fingers that had burrowed in her hair now cupped her chin. "The style's all wrong for you."

To Haley's dismay, the small erotic frisson she had felt moments before had intensified, the spot where his flesh made contact with hers becoming a source of tremendous warmth. Unwillingly, she became aware of the lean, hard strength of Adam's body as he stood so close beside her, trapping her back casually against the counter. Quickly, furtively, her eyes searched his, seeking evidence that he, too, was aware of the heat generated between them, but she found none. His smoky gaze was as friendly, as guileless, as open, as ever.

My God, what am I thinking? she wondered, utterly unnerved by her body's response. Fluidly, she twisted free, then turned, moving away down the counter to busy herself with the coffee maker.

"I don't see why you don't like it," she remarked, pleased that the steadiness of her voice gave nothing away. "Lots of women wear their hair curly. It's very much the style. Besides," she added, goaded by a sudden need to erect some barriers between them, "Cliff loves it this way."

"Cliff also loves madras pants and Richard Nixon," Adam pointed out grimly. "So don't try holding him up to me as an arbiter of good taste. You're not lots of women, Haley. You're you—different and utterly unique." He paused, and when he spoke again, the words were said so softly that Haley almost didn't hear them. "With that thick black mane hanging halfway down your back, you look sleek and exotic, almost primitive— like a wild, graceful jungle cat."

Her back still turned as she filled his mug with hot coffee, Haley glowed with sudden pleasure, the words washing over her like a soft caress. All at once, the warmth she had felt earlier at his touch was nothing compared to the shiver of delight that flamed her senses now. Was that really how he saw her? she wondered, finding herself utterly enchanted by the fanciful image.

Her eyes luminous with pleasure, Haley swung around to face him. No sooner had she done so, however, than the bubble quickly burst, for immediately she saw that Adam's features were carefully schooled into a polite mask of bland indifference; the gaze that roamed down over her slender figure possessed a clinical, assessing intent and nothing more. A sharp stab of disappointment pierced through her as, belatedly, Haley realized that the beauty of Adam's compliment probably owed more to his writer's flair for graceful phrasing than to any eloquence she herself had inspired within him. Frowning, she shoved the mug into his outstretched hand.

"But this," Adam continued, gesturing derisively at her headful of curls, "this doesn't suit you at all."

"Maybe not," Haley allowed with a small, careless shrug,

unwilling to let him see the effect his casual words had had on her equilibrium. "But I'm afraid it's too late to do anything about it now—"

"Good God, you're right!" Adam barked, his eyes seeking out the time on the slim gold watch on his wrist. "Scoot!" he ordered. Propelling her toward the bedroom door, he sent her on her way with a stinging slap to her rear end. "And for God's sake, woman, be quick about it!"

In her room, Haley made short work of the remaining preparations, her stocking-clad toes finding the missing shoe and slipping it on while her fingers quickly raked through the curls, taming them into place.

Talk about letting yourself get carried away! she thought, grimacing at her reflection in the mirror. What on earth could she have been thinking to respond to Adam like that? He was her pal, her buddy, her partner, for Pete's sake! Besides, it wasn't as if he'd never paid her a compliment before. He had, many times, the subjects of his admiration ranging from her clear, concise writing to a brilliantly executed end play during a tough slam contract in bridge. But this time, she mused uneasily, there had been a difference.

Or had there? she wondered, picking up her lipstick and quickly outlining her lips with a deep, clear shade of red. Maybe she was simply making too much out of nothing. Was it her fault she'd always been a sucker for a well-turned phrase? Damn T. J., anyway, for putting all those romantic ideas in her head! They were fine in theory, but in practice—

"Haley!" His tone was not one you would want to hear twice.

"Coming!" she yelled back, snatching up her purse and the linen jacket that lay draped across her still-rumpled bed. She dashed out into the living room to find the front door standing open and Adam already outside. Hastily, she followed, pulling the door shut and locking it behind her.

"What a glorious morning!" she enthused, pausing by the

side of the cottage to look out over the Sound and breathe in the fresh, salt-tinged air.

"Some of us," Adam said meaningfully, "are in too much of a hurry to notice."

"Pity," Haley commented as he linked his arm firmly through hers, leading her across the driveway toward his sleek burgundy-colored Datsun 280ZX. "You know, you ought to let yourself enjoy life more. All that worrying's going to give you ulcers."

"If I get ulcers," Adam replied, "I'll know exactly who gave them to me. Do you realize that you've left us with exactly twelve minutes to make a ten-minute drive?"

"No problem," Haley assured him airily. "I don't know who taught you how to subtract, but the way I see it, we've got two minutes to spare."

"Only because I got here early this morning and lit a fire under you," Adam pointed out.

Briefly, Haley's eyes widened as she contemplated the truth behind his innocent words. Adam, however, seemed totally oblivious, and with a small shake of her head, she thrust the thought aside.

"So that's what you were doing, trying to move up my timetable?" she said, pretending to pout, "and here I'd thought you came early because you couldn't wait another minute for my sparkling company."

"A gentleman never tells," Adam retorted with a cheeky grin.

"How would you know?" Haley teased. Reaching the burgundy Zee, she unlinked her arm from his and continued on, walking past it.

Behind her, Adam stopped, planted his hands on his hips and sighed with exasperation. "Now where do you think you're going?"

"To the car, of course," Haley replied blithely, heading toward the small white convertible Rabbit that was her pride and joy.

"The *wrong* car," Adam said smoothly, preparing himself for a fight. Since both were enthusiastic drivers, it was a disagreement they'd had many times in the past.

"Not at all," said Haley. "On a beautiful morning such as this, how can you even think of cooping yourself up indoors? My car," she pointed out needlessly, "has the advantage of open-air styling."

"My car," Adam said firmly as he strode forward to claim her arm once more, "has the advantage of me driving it."

"Are you saying you don't like the way I drive?"

"Not at all; you're a fine driver."

"But?" Haley prompted, waiting for the other shoe to drop.

"But," Adam said mildly, "I don't see any reason why you should exercise your skills when I'm around to do it for you."

"I don't want my driving done for me!" Haley cried, infuriated by his tone of calm superiority.

"Haley," Adam said quietly, his tone growing calmer even as hers grew more shrill, "as you yourself pointed out, we only have two minutes to spare in our drive over to the hardware store. No doubt this discussion has already used up one of them, and I have no desire to waste the other as well. Now either you are going to move your tail and get into this car, or I am going to pick you up and put you in."

"There you go again, turning all macho on me." Haley sighed. "Can I help it if you have a hangup about always needing to be in charge?"

"What's wrong with that? As the man around here, I should be in charge."

"Talk about Neanderthal ideas!" Haley cried, outraged.

"Is that what we were talking about?" Adam inquired innocently. "Funny, I thought we were discussing the infuriating habit you have of always being late."

"Oh, for Pete's sake!" Haley groaned, rolling her eyes heavenward. Trying to shake Adam loose from something he wanted was like trying to pry a bone out of the jaws of a hungry bulldog. "How about this?" she proposed, her tawny eyes snapping defiantly. "You can drive—but *only* on the condition that you promise not to say another word about what time it is."

"Done," Adam agreed with a quick, self-satisfied grin. Pivoting on his heel, he strode back to the waiting Zee, leaving Haley to follow along in his wake.

Damn! she thought, strolling along behind. He'd done it to her again! How was it that this man found her so infuriatingly easy to get around?

With Adam behind the wheel, exercising the sports car's powerful motor to its full potential, they made it to the hardware store with at least thirty seconds to spare before the appointed hour.

"See?" Haley declared as she unfastened her seat belt and climbed out of the low car. "I told you we'd make it." She walked around and opened the hatchback, then hoisted out one of several boxes filled with books that they had brought with them to sell.

"So you did," Adam conceded with a smile, "although you never mentioned that you meant to cheerlead me into breaking every speed limit between here and Greenwich, running three red lights in the process. Lady, as back-seat drivers go, you're a maniac!"

"So we broke a few rules," she said with a careless shrug. "I won't tell if you won't."

"My lips are sealed," Adam vowed, and they grinned at one another happily.

Inside the store, the manager was waiting. They had met several weeks earlier when the idea had first been proposed and accepted, then once again when Adam and Haley had stopped by to drop off a large sign promoting their upcoming appearance. Now, as they followed him to the back of the first floor where the plumbing supplies were sold, Haley noted with satisfaction that everything seemed to be in readiness.

A large space had been cleared and a table set up on which they were to display their books. Two straight-backed chairs were in place behind it, while on top were a cup containing half a dozen pens and pencils and a pitcher filled with cool water. Not only that, but above their heads hung a banner, strung from one end of the store to the other, proclaiming their names and the title of their book.

"Goodness!" Haley exclaimed under her breath, casting a nervous glance out of the corner of her eye at Adam. "I wasn't expecting all this. He's gone to so much trouble. What are we going to do if nobody shows up?"

"Don't worry," Adam assured her as he set the box of books he was carrying down on the long table and began to unpack them. "They'll come."

And come they did. All morning long, the back of the store hummed with activity as people came and went by the carload. Haley, who had expected to sign no more than a dozen books or so, found her fingers growing cramped and then numb as they went quickly through the first box of books, then moved on to the second. Through it all, she smiled and chatted, handling one side of the room while Adam took the other, fielding questions about everything from how to work with copper tubing to the cheapest and most efficient way to install a sump pump.

Thank God they had done their research thoroughly! she thought when several hours had come and gone and still the crowds showed no sign of letting up. Honestly, whoever would have thought there were so many home handymen? And all of them wanting to compare notes on the repairs and innovations they had made to their own plumbing. It was mind boggling!

"How are you holding up?" came a warm, familiar voice in her ear, and Haley turned to find Adam standing beside her.

"Fine, I think," she said with a smile, "although some of these men have really put me through the wringer. From the questions they're asking, I get the distinct impression they'd like to trip me up."

"You can handle them," said Adam, patting her shoulder lightly. "I'm sure you're doing great. After all, you know more about plumbing than any other woman I know."

"Big deal," Haley sniffed, though inwardly she was grateful for his confidence. "I've seen the women you hang out with, and that's roughly equivalent to being called the best water-skier in all of Death Valley. Nice, but there's not much competition for the job, if you see what I mean."

"Oh, I don't know," Adam said with a broad wink and a lewd grin. "You remember Annabelle, don't you? Now that was one woman who really knew how to make the most of good plumbing. Why she knew more ways to get creative with bath oil—"

"No fair!" Haley laughed, brushing his example aside. "I'm talking under the tub, not in it!"

Looking over his shoulder, she nodded toward a group of women who had just entered the store and were trying to attract his attention. "Your adoring public awaits, Mr. Bubbles. I think you'd better get back to work."

As soon as he left her side, Haley was approached by a tall, sandy-haired man sporting a large paunch, a pair of patched blue jeans and a faded work shirt with the sleeves rolled up to reveal his brawny forearms. "Where's this guy Morgan at, anyway?" he demanded. "I got Burke's signature in the book already, but I want to get them both."

"I'm Morgan," said Haley in a tone that she hoped denoted quiet authority. She stepped forward and extended her hand, somewhat dismayed to find that she stood at eye level with the third button on the man's shirt. "I'd be happy to sign your book for you."

"You?" He laughed derisively, ignoring her outstretched hand. "Hell, I'm not looking to have my book signed by no secretary. Get me that other writer, what's-his-name."

"Perhaps you didn't hear what I said," Haley said coolly. "I *am* Haley Morgan, the coauthor."

As he looked down at her, the man's eyes narrowed speculatively. His gaze roamed over her from head to toe in insolent appraisal. "You're the other guy that wrote the book?" he demanded, his tone clearly conveying his disbelief.

Silently, Haley nodded, not quite sure if she trusted herself to give a civil answer. Concentrating on the task, she counted slowly to ten before looking up to meet his gaze once more.

"Well, I'll be damned," the man swore, scratching his head.

"Now, then," Haley said evenly, having finished her counting, "would you like me to sign your book?"

She reached out her hand to take the copy from him, but instead of handing over the book, the man grasped her wrist and used the hold to draw her closer. "Come on," he prompted in a low, conspiratorial tone that Haley found incredibly irritating, "you can level with me. What do you really do for that guy Burke? I mean, he may have let you have your name on the cover of the book, but that still don't convince me that a pretty little thing like you would know the difference between a hacksaw and an offset wrench."

Bristling inwardly, Haley forced herself to remain calm, the only outward evidence of her anger being the slight flare of her tightly pinched nostrils. "I assure you," she said firmly, twisting out of his grasp, "Adam and I contributed equally to the finished manuscript. In fact, we worked on it together side by side for over half a year."

At that, the man's eyes lit up lewdly in his florid face. "I'm sure you did, honey."

As far as Haley was concerned, the patronizing quality in his tone was the last straw. "What's that supposed to mean?" she hissed from between tightly clenched teeth.

"Now, now, don't get all riled up," the man said placatingly. "Hell, I'm not saying you're not good at what you do. Why, you can help me write a book anytime." Reaching out, he stroked her curls with the tips of his work-stained fingers, and immediately Haley stiffened with outrage. "Honey, I'll bet in your case, the collaborating's what makes it all worthwhile."

It had been years since Haley'd been genuinely shocked enough by anything to blush, and she was uncertain whether the dull red flush that crept up over her cheeks owed more to the degrading insinuation of his words or to the anger that was no longer in check and was bubbling dangerously close to the surface.

Whoever said the customer is always right had a few choice things to learn about human nature, she thought irrelevantly, just as this man had a few things to learn about good manners. Things she would be only too glad to teach him!

"Now you listen here, buddy——!"

The first inkling Haley had that someone had come up behind her came when her shoulders were firmly grasped and she found herself being nudged to one side. Sensing another challenge but not yet discerning its source, she broke off in midsentence, struggling instinctively against her unknown captor.

"Shh," said Adam, his voice calm, yet decisive. "I'll handle this."

Her adrenalin was racing along at top speed, and Haley's mind immediately formed a protest, but before there was time to utter the words, Adam had placed her aside, then moved so as to place himself between Haley and the man who had accosted her, his body assuming a stance of belligerent menace. "Now, then," he said, his voice ominously quiet, "I believe you owe the lady an apology."

"Hey—listen—er, I didn't mean anything by it," the man stammered. Though he must have outweighed Adam easily, one look told him that he was no match for the fit, well-toned author, and he squirmed visibly beneath Adam's angry glare. "I mean, how was I to know she was private property——"

"The apology," Adam repeated, his tone brooking no argument. With a quick glance down at Haley, the man complied before backing away hastily to become lost in the crowd.

It wasn't until he was gone that Haley realized she had been holding her breath, but now it all escaped in one long whoosh. "Are you all right?" Adam asked quietly, looking down over her from head to toe as if to assure himself that all was well.

"Fine," Haley snapped, finding that her anger was not at all mitigated by the resolution of the scene. In fact, if anything, it was growing, and she directed the full force of her wrath toward the man who had come to her rescue. "I'm fine," she repeated once more, "and not only that, I was *doing* fine. I'm perfectly capable of taking care of myself, you know. How dare you treat me like that?"

"Not now," Adam growled under his breath. Glancing up, Haley immediately realized the reason for his reticence, for they were being watched with avid interest by several pairs of curious eyes.

"Later, then," she promised in a discreet undertone, and Adam nodded curtly before turning away to resume his job.

Smiling outwardly, Haley forced herself once more back into the role of the charming coauthor, but inside she was a mass of seething emotion. Throughout the rest of the morning, she forgot neither her anger nor its source; the thought of Adam's intervention, no matter how well meaning, pricked like a thorn in her side, one that had been there for quite some time.

Would he never stop thinking of her as a child? she wondered crossly. The man who'd harassed her was a bully, true, but she could have handled him. Perhaps with less dispatch than Adam had shown but still with an ample measure of *adult* proficiency. But no, Adam hadn't trusted that she would be able to look out for herself. Instead, he'd stepped in and taken charge, as he always did, without once stopping to consider whether or not she even wanted help. Well, that was the last time he was going to get away with that! she decided firmly. And as soon as they got home, she would tell him so.

The appearance, which was to have ended at noon, dragged on until nearly one; finally, the last of the customers who had come to meet them was satisfied. The ride back to Haley's house was accomplished in a chilly, uncomfortable silence, with Adam devoting his full attention to his driving and Haley staring pointedly out the window.

Guessing that he hoped to get away with dropping her off at her door and then leaving, she forestalled that cowardly act by motioning his car into the parking space next to her Rabbit. "Oh, no, you don't!" Haley announced. "You're not getting out of this one quite so easily. You and I have got some talking to do!"

Preceding him inside, she shrugged out of her linen jacket, then flung it down, along with her purse, onto the nearest chair. "Just what," she demanded, "did you think you were doing?"

With calm deliberation, Adam closed the door behind him, then took off his own jacket as well and laid it neatly over the back of the couch. Plunging his hands deep into the pockets of his trousers, he turned and faced her across the small room. "All I was trying to do," he said slowly, "was help you out of a potentially unpleasant situation."

"You mean all you were trying to do was run my life!"

Glaring at her, Adam frowned. "Maybe you need someone to run your life," he growled. "Sometimes I think you're too damned independent for your own good."

"Of course I'm independent!" Haley cried. "Why shouldn't I be? After all, I'm an adult. I've been fighting my own battles for years now." Her hands balled into fists of impotent rage at her sides. "Look at me, Adam," she invited, wanting him to see her as she really was. "I may not be very big, but I *am* all grown up."

"I know that," Adam replied coolly.

"Then start treating me that way!"

"I do," he said simply.

"Not this morning you didn't." Haley shook her head. "You treated me like a child who couldn't be trusted to take care of herself. I'm not your little sister, you know."

For a moment, there was only silence as Adam's eyes flickered over her briefly, alight with an emotion that Haley could not identify. "I'm aware of that," he said deeply, his anger rising to match her own. "Believe me, Haley, there is nothing fraternal about the way I feel toward you right now!"

"Oh?" she replied, knowing she was baiting him but unable to stop herself. "And how is that?"

"Right now," Adam grated, "I would take enormous pleasure in turning you over my knee and knocking some sense into you."

"You wouldn't dare," Haley scoffed, but as Adam glowered angrily, crossing the room in three quick strides, her dark eyes widened in alarm.

"Don't push your luck," he growled, "because believe me, lady, where you're concerned, there are a lot of things I'd dare."

He came to a stop less than a yard away. Hastily, Haley restrained her first reaction, which was to bolt, to back away until she had once more put a safe distance between them. His anger, combined now with the proximity of his taut, well-muscled body, made her restless and edgy in a way that had the hackles on the back of her neck rising in alarm. She was responding to him again—not in anger or in fear but in the elemental way that a woman responds to a man she wants—and she knew it. Immediately, instinctively, she denied her attraction, turning her anger and confusion into defiance instead.

"Just because we're old friends, Adam, doesn't mean that I'm going to let you manhandle me!"

Glancing down over her diminutive form, bristling now with outrage but still somewhat less than formidable, Adam couldn't suppress a smile. "Who says I need your permission?" he asked pleasantly.

"Ooh!" Haley gritted her teeth in helpless fury. Spinning on her heel, she strode across the room to the picture window that faced out over the terrace and the water beyond. Hugging her arms tightly across her chest, she stared at the panoramic view without seeing any of it; for the second time that day, she found herself wondering what in the world was going on between them. She and Adam never fought like this. In the past, when they'd disagreed about something, they'd discussed their differences calmly and rationally, not yelled at each other from across the room like two hooligans!

No, thought Haley, she knew Adam well enough to realize that that day's angry, emotional outburst was as foreign to his nature as it was to her own. So what was the matter with the two of them? Why, suddenly, was there friction between them, a vague, impalpable feeling of tension that had never been there before? Adam must feel it, too, she realized. Was he as confused as she was?

With a small inward sigh, Haley accepted that she had no answers. In fact, at that moment, there was only one thing she *was* sure of—Adam was her friend, her best friend, and the feelings she had for him were much too precious to be jeopardized by some silly spat.

She was so wrapped up in her own thoughts, that it was a moment before Haley realized that Adam had followed her across the room and was now standing beside the window next to her, sharing the contemplative silence. He seemed to sense, however, the moment that she became aware of his presence, for he looked over at her and smiled. "Independence is a fine thing," he said softly, "but I've found that sometimes it helps just to have someone to lean on."

Smiling tremulously in return, Haley accepted the overture for what it was—an affirmation that their friendship was still very much intact. Then, cocking her head to one side, she squinted up at him playfully. "Does this mean that you're offering yourself for the job?"

For a moment, Haley was afraid she'd made another mistake, for the deep gray eyes that gazed down at her were suddenly fathomless and totally unreadable. "And if I am?"

Why was he looking at her like that? she wondered, her heart constricting painfully within her breast. Was it her imagination, or was there more to the simple offer than could be read at face value . . . ? No! her thoughts screamed abruptly in frantic denial. She was getting carried away again, and she wasn't going to let that happen!

When she replied a moment later, her tone, though sincere, was deliberately light. "Oh, Adam, you make a wonderful knight in shining armor. I'm only sorry that I didn't do a better job as the fair damsel." Goaded by a spontaneous impulse that refused to be denied, Haley launched herself forward, wrapping her arms tightly around Adam's neck and hugging him to her. "I'm touched that you came to my defense; really, I am."

Adam drew his head back to gaze down at her searchingly, as though there were something he wanted to say. Then his expression changed, and the moment was gone. Setting her down on the ground, he continued on with the downward motion to form a mockingly courtly bow. "Anytime, milady," he replied formally. "Your wish is my command."

"Hmm," Haley said with a grin, stroking her chin thoughtfully as she considered the wealth of possibility laid open by that offer. Then, laughing, she reached out to trail her finger down the picture window beside them, leaving a long, dusty streak in its wake. "Do you by any chance do windows?"

3

~oooooooooo~

That evening, dressing for her date, Haley was determined not to be late. Cliff was much more lenient in such matters than Adam, but still it was a bad habit, one that she was trying to mend. Besides, she told herself, they would be driving directly from her house to the small French restaurant in Westport where they were meeting Adam and Sheila, so any delay on her part was sure to be noticed.

Tying her hair up on top of her head, she showered quickly, then cleared the steam off the bathroom mirror with a few broad strokes of her hand so that she could lean forward over the sink and apply her makeup. Rich bronze eye shadow deepened and darkened her eyes, followed by a generous coating of black mascara, thicker on the outer lashes to open her wide-set eyes still farther. A delicate peach blusher, applied high on her cheekbones, warmed the honey tones of her skin, and she finished by filling in her lips with a muted shade of coral gloss.

Unwrapping the towel from her now dry body, Haley hung it on the rack beside the door, then sauntered out into her bedroom naked. Absently, she reached up to undo the pins that held her hair in place, and it tumbled down about her shoulders in a cascade of soft, rippling waves, the effect of the long day and the steamy shower having subdued the riotous curls to a more manageable state. Coming upon her reflection suddenly in the full-length mirror on the back of her closet door, she hesitated, then stopped, frowning thoughtfully at the image.

A jungle cat? she mused whimsically, pleased by the new perception of herself but not at all sure that it was accurate. Was that really how Adam saw her, as something wild and sleek and exotic?

She turned first one way, then the other, studying her body without self-consciousness but with a fair amount of critical acumen. Perhaps her slim, streamlined figure could be considered sleek, she decided. Stretching her arms up over her head experimentally, she undulated her body in an imitation of feline languor and grace. But *exotic?*

Biting down on her lower lip, Haley sighed. That unexpected comment of Adam's was only one of several things during the past few weeks that she hadn't understood—like his insistence on writing a romance when always before their topics had been chosen by mutual consent; his overreaction that morning to the bully in the hardware store; and worst of all, her continuing overreactions to him. What was happening between the two of them, anyway?

Suddenly, everything seemed to be changing, shifting into new patterns in a way that left her feeling restless and edgy and more than a little uncomfortable. In the past, they'd always been totally open with one another, sharing their thoughts, their feelings, their dreams. Yet now that sense of easiness that she had come to take for granted seemed to be slipping away, overshadowed by a vague undercurrent of tension that modified their relationship in all sorts of unexpected ways.

Starting a new project was always difficult, but this time something was different, something that went beyond the normal everyday problems engendered by their working together. Because no matter how badly the work had gone in the past, they'd always been careful not to allow those feelings to spill over into their relationship. The two things had been kept totally separate. Now, however, Haley was not at all sure that was still the case. No, she felt the change, she sensed it happening, and the specter of it hung over their friendship like the pallor of impending doom.

Was it her fault? she wondered. Was it Adam's? Or perhaps, she mused fancifully, was it the fault of the romance that they were writing? She'd always been one to throw herself into her work heart and soul. Could it be that this time she had gone too far? By wallowing in romantic fantasies for the sake of the novel, was it possible that she had immersed herself so thoroughly in the character that she'd even begun to accept some of Allegra's emotions as her own?

Certainly she'd never been so physically aware of Adam as a man as she had been during the past two weeks, since they started the book. Indeed, after all these years, she had thought herself quite immune to his virile brand of attraction. Yet suddenly, time and again, she was being supplied with ample proof that she was not, her body responding quite unexpectedly to every shade and nuance of his behavior. Just as, if her memory served her correctly, Allegra was finally beginning to open up and respond to Rex!

The taut muscles rippled smoothly over her slender frame as Haley arched her back suddenly, rolling her shoulders forward and curling her fingers into long, dangerous-looking claws. "Meeeow!" she snarled, hissing playfully at the image in the mirror and destroying the illusion.

That had to be it, Haley decided, and now that she knew what was going on, she could fight it—keep Allegra and her emotions confined to the printed page, where they belonged. Thank God she'd figured out what was the matter before things had gotten out of hand, she thought with a heartfelt sigh of relief. Because if Adam, sweet, wonderful, good-buddy Adam, had ever realized what kind of thoughts she'd been entertaining on his behalf, she would never have been able to live it down!

Her problems solved for the time being, Haley hurried to finish getting ready, but unfortunately, the long, reflective discourse that had straightened out her life also had the unwelcome result of making her late once more. Though she raced around the bedroom with the speed of the possessed, dressing quickly in a slinky black halter-neck jump suit that had always been one of her favorites, Cliff still ended up cooling his heels for several minutes in the living room while she found her shoes, slipped on some jewelry and applied the finishing touches.

Then, while Haley gritted her teeth in helpless frustration, he drove slowly and carefully, as was his style, to the small French restaurant on the outskirts of Westport. Though new, it was already renowned for its fine continental cuisine and the quality of the dance band that played after dinner on Friday and Saturday nights, the crowded parking lot they found on their arrival attesting to its popularity. After turning the car over to the valet, Haley linked her arm through Cliff's and hurried him inside. Nevertheless, by the time they arrived, Adam and Sheila were not only already seated at their table but also, from the looks of the half-empty glasses before them, finishing their first drinks as well.

"Don't tell me; let me guess," said Adam, standing up as they approached. "You two had car trouble? Got lost, perhaps? No, neither of the above?" His gray eyes glittered mischievously. "Then, in that case, there's only one reason I can think of why you'd be so late. . . ."

He looked pointedly in Haley's direction, and she returned his glare with interest before shooting a quick glance out of the corner of her eye at Cliff, hoping for some moral support. To her surprise, however, she found that he was totally oblivious to the conversation at hand, all his attention focused instead on Sheila, the fourth member of their party, whom he had yet to meet. A woman of delicate, Madonnalike beauty, Sheila had pale, almost translucent ivory skin, artfully tousled auburn hair and a body that could stop traffic. She had remained seated as they approached, and now she smiled up at Cliff warmly, her most visible assets displayed to distinct advantage in a charmingly low-cut peasant blouse.

Staring over at her date perplexedly, Haley followed the line of his gaze and saw that from where they stood, the slight tilt of his head had given Cliff a direct view downward into Sheila's considerable cleavage, a sight that he was enjoying to its full potential.

"I don't believe you two have met," Adam said smoothly. Haley glanced back up to find that his lips were twitching with barely suppressed humor. Catching her eye, he dropped one lid in an audacious wink before turning to perform the introductions.

"I'm ever so pleased to meet you," Sheila cooed delightedly.

"Believe me, the pleasure is all mine," said Cliff, his hazel eyes alight with appreciation.

Mouth regrettably agape, Haley watched his reaction with disbelief. Was this the quiet, ultraconservative attorney she'd come with? Could this possibly be the same man who had known her for months before getting up the nerve to ask her out and then staunchly refused to kiss on the first date?

As if he'd totally forgotten her presence, Cliff slid down into the chair beside Sheila, leaving Haley, who by this time was quite speechless, to find her own seat. The reaction that came from her other side sounded suspiciously like a chuckle, but when she whipped around, her dark eyes shooting fire, Adam was only clearing his throat, his face wearing quite the phoniest expression of innocence Haley had ever seen. Without saying a word, he stepped in to fill the breach; equally silent, she accepted the chair he politely offered and sat.

Terrific, she thought, groaning inwardly as words like short, skinny and flat as a board ran full tilt through her head. What was it about the presence of a truly impressive set of mammary glands that had the effect of turning normal, thinking men into a collection of blithering idiots? Couldn't they see anything past the obvious?

Adam signaled over the waiter, and they ordered a round of drinks; then Sheila turned to Haley with an artless smile. "It's so nice to see you again," she said warmly. "How have you been?"

"Just fine," Haley replied automatically. "How about you?"

Too bad she was nice on top of everything else, Haley thought irritably. It would be so much easier to dislike Sheila if the woman was a real witch. But she wasn't, not at all. Though Haley privately suspected that thinking had never been her strong point, she was gentle and kind—if often somewhat out of touch with reality. The last of the flower children, Adam had called her once, and he'd been right. With her flowing red hair, her voluptuously unbound figure and her penchant for dressing in gypsy clothing, she was a free spirit and, for all her twenty-five years, an innocent child who had yet to grow up.

"Oh, I'm just fine," Sheila replied happily. She leaned closer across the table, and her breasts strained against the thin, gauzy material that contained them in a way that had Cliff's eyes bulging from their sockets. "And I want to hear all about your new book. Before you arrived, Adam was telling me that the two of you are doing a romance this time. I think that sounds terribly exciting. I can't wait to read it!"

"Good," Haley said with a grin. "That's one copy sold."

"And you said we'd never be able to make a success of this thing," Adam chided her teasingly.

"No, I didn't," Haley cried. "I only—"

"So tell me, Sheila, what do you do?" Cliff broke in as though she hadn't even been speaking at all.

Turning to glare at him in outrage, Haley realized suddenly from the rapt expression on his face that he probably wasn't even aware of interrupting her. He wasn't being rude, merely oblivious, for as far as he was concerned, she might as well have vanished altogether. Good grief! she thought in dismay, her pride thoroughly dented by the turn of events. Granted, she and Cliff were hardly the last of the red-hot lovers, but still it was more than a little demoralizing to have her date jump ship so readily. And with such apparent relish for his new port of call!

What in the world must Adam be thinking of all this? she wondered suddenly, glancing furtively in his direction and steeling herself against the gleam of mocking amusement she was sure she would find in his eyes. To her surprise, however, he did not meet her gaze at all. His expression was reflective and rather remote as he listened, along with Cliff, to Sheila's animated description of her job as the counter girl in a local nursery.

Leaning back in her chair, Haley sipped thoughtfully at her gin and tonic, her dark eyes darting back and forth between Cliff, who sat to her right, and Adam, who was on her left. Unwittingly, without even realizing what she was doing, she began to draw comparisons between the two men.

Both were in their early thirties, both handsome, self-assured and quite successful in their chosen professions; but there the similarities stopped. Seeing them both together, Haley was struck by a blandness in Cliff's appearance that she had not noticed before; a softness that had nothing to do with the muscle tone of the fit, athletic body that he so painstakingly maintained. No, it was rather something about the set of his chin that, she saw by comparison, lacked Adam's stubborn thrust of determination or the posture with which he held himself, properly straight and erect, yet somehow not imposing. From the top of his carefully styled wheat-blond hair to the tips of his brown Gucci loafers, he was impeccably turned out and utterly correct, yet somehow lacking in the commanding presence that, even in a roomful of successful men, still set Adam apart.

With a quick, negative shake of her head, Haley banished her disloyal thoughts. Just because Cliff was in the process of falling all over another man's date while supposedly being her own was no reason to think such things about him behind his back! Then again, said a small voice inside her head, if that isn't a good reason to turn on a man, what is?

In spite of herself, that thought made her grin wickedly, and feeling much better, she put down her drink and turned back into the conversation. The talk had now progressed from the nursery where Sheila worked to the subject of plants in general, and Haley watched with something akin to admiration as the other woman flirted with the two men, preening prettily as though it were second nature to her. No doubt, Haley decided, because it was.

". . . and they grow ever so much better if you talk to them," Sheila was explaining happily. "Actually, singing's even better. It seems to make them happy, you know."

"How interesting," Cliff murmured, and Haley guessed that in his neat, orderly mind, he was filing away plans to go out and purchase a plant on Monday.

"Haley had a plant once, didn't you?" Adam said from across the table, his gray eyes glinting mischievously.

"Just one?" cried Sheila, her lips pursing in a charmingly delicate pout. "But they won't thrive that way. Plants are very sociable creatures."

"Not this one." Haley laughed. "It was a cactus, and totally antisocial. It pricked anything and everything."

"With all the beautiful plants there are to choose from, why on earth did you get a cactus?" said Cliff, frowning impatiently.

"Actually, I wasn't the one who chose it," Haley admitted, warming to the tale. "It was a gift from my mother. She loves plants, and when I was growing up, our house was always filled with them; but it didn't take long for me to become known as the one member of the family with a black thumb. Every plant I ever had always turned brown and died."

"Somehow Haley's haphazard style of housekeeping never seemed to allow for living things, such as plants, that needed to be watered regularly and on schedule," Adam interjected with a grin.

"I can see why you had a problem," Sheila murmured sympathetically.

"I don't remember ever seeing your cactus," Cliff remarked thoughtfully. He paused, then added, "Although I must admit I have noticed your disregard for some of the finer points of housekeeping."

"I don't have it anymore," Haley confessed, replying to the first part of his comment and pointedly ignoring the second.

Cliff might forgive her tendency toward tardiness, but he was considerably less-lenient when it came to such things as old newspapers, unmade beds and dirty dishes stacked in the sink for later.

"But they're practically foolproof," Sheila pointed out. "No matter how many times you forget to water a cactus, they never die."

"Yes, I know," Haley admitted, hoping that she injected the proper amount of wistful regret into her voice.

"So what ever happened to it?" Cliff's tone clearly insinuated his wish that she get on with it.

"I was moving the furniture around one day," said Haley, then paused melodramatically for effect, "and I tripped and dropped a chair on it, thereby bringing its short but happy life to an untimely end."

"Oh, that's terrible!" Sheila squealed, giggling delightedly at the outcome, her laughter so infectious that the others couldn't help but join in.

The waiter appeared to deliver another round of drinks and hand out the menus, then hovered unobtrusively in the background while they made their selections. Adam and Cliff ordered the prime rib, while Haley and Sheila both opted for veal cordon bleu, which was the house specialty.

"I understand you're a lawyer," said Sheila, turning to Cliff when the waiter had disappeared once more. "I want you to know that I've read everything Erle Stanley Gardner ever wrote, and I think Perry Mason was just wonderful."

"Well, actually," Cliff said slowly, "I'm not a criminal lawyer like Perry Mason was. My specialty is tax law."

"Oh?" Sheila's green eyes widened. "Does that mean you do people's taxes for them, just like H and R Block?"

"Not exactly," Cliff hedged, and Haley quickly suppressed a giggle at the pained expression that crossed his face. He looked wounded to the very core at the thought of his esteemed profession being likened to that of a street-corner franchise.

Well, if it was any comfort to him, thought Haley, she could sympathize with how he felt. Somehow things weren't going at all the way she had planned, either. After T. J.'s apt assessment, she'd expected to spend the evening running interference between two people who couldn't begin to understand one another and had no desire to try. And to think, she'd been afraid that with nothing in common, they'd have nothing to say! If the expression on Cliff's face was anything to go by, words were proving entirely unnecessary. He and Sheila were on a wavelength all their own.

Over dinner, the conversation became more general, their topics running the gamut from sports to politics to the latest Broadway show. Although Haley never succeeded in capturing Cliff's full attention, she did score several points in the midst of a lively debate over local elections, which seemed to have the effect of reminding him, however briefly, that she was still alive.

If she hadn't been so directly involved in the whole debacle, Haley decided over dessert, she would actually have thought that it was quite funny. Cliff was the last person she'd have suspected would be bowled over by Sheila's charms, yet from all appearances, he was quite smitten—absolutely besotted to the point where he didn't care who knew about it. Unfortunately, however, she was involved. It was her pride that was on the line and her dignity that was in the process of being thoroughly affronted. Granted, Sheila was a beautiful woman, she thought, watching Cliff's eyes follow the other woman's movements as she slowly licked a dollop of ice cream off her spoon, but she wasn't the only woman at the table!

With a slight, almost imperceptible movement, Haley squared her shoulders. She was a fighter, not a quitter, and she quickly squelched any niggling doubts over whether or not the prize might be worth the effort. There were principles at stake here—hers!

"Tell me, Cliff," she said, reaching out to place her hand on his arm and drawing his attention back to her corner. "How is your work on the planning and zoning commission coming? Are you still debating the extent to which commercial development should be allowed to continue?"

It was a controversial topic, Haley knew, and one that was guaranteed to produce spirited discussion, as Cliff was well known for being in favor of the increased industry, which brought more tax money into the town coffers, while Adam was just as vehemently opposed to expansion, declaring that the preservation of the community's small-town atmosphere was the issue of paramount importance.

"Just look at Long Island Sound and the beaches," said Adam. "You can see what effect increased commerce is having on them in terms of pollution!"

"Nevertheless," Cliff maintained, "those companies which have moved their corporate headquarters here are paying tax money whose benefit to the town cannot be ignored."

"You know, you're both right," Haley interjected, "and you're both wrong as well. You"—she looked over at Cliff—"for being too mercenary and not taking the long-term view. And you"—she swung her head around to look at Adam—"for wanting to stand in the way of progress."

"Oh, I'm all in favor of progress . . ." Adam fired back quickly.

"I know, I know." Haley laughed, guessing what was coming next. "As long as they do it in somebody else's town, right?"

"Exactly." Adam grinned.

"What do you think, Sheila?" Cliff asked, and all eyes turned to focus on the only one not to offer an opinion thus far.

"Well," Sheila said slowly, twirling her finger through her long auburn tresses as she thought. "I suppose it's a shame that nobody wants to go swimming in the Sound anymore."

Ignoring Adam's satisfied nod, Cliff pressed the point further. "Yes, of course, but do you feel that the corporations which have brought more industry to the area ought to be held responsible?"

This time, Sheila was silent for almost a full minute. Then she looked around the table, her large green eyes open wide with confusion as she settled for lifting her creamy shoulders in a dainty shrug.

"Wonderful!" cried Cliff, clapping his hands delightedly. "Sheila, you're a born diplomat!"

That's not the word I would have chosen, Haley thought grumpily.

At that moment, their discussion was brought to an end by the sound of several instruments being tuned up in the alcove off the dining room, alerting them to the fact that it was time for the band to begin playing. As soon as the combo swung into their first number, Adam rose from the table and extended his hand to Sheila, leading her off toward the small parquet dance floor.

Had he finally decided it was time to restake his claim? Haley wondered moodily, frowning at this unwelcome reminder that the other woman had not one but both of the men at the table wrapped neatly around her little finger. Talk about being a fifth wheel, she mused as Cliff's eyes wistfully followed the pair away. She had never felt so totally expendable in her entire life!

"Wow," Cliff murmured under his breath, swinging back around to Haley as the pair disappeared around the corner. "That Sheila is really something else."

"Yes," Haley agreed with a weary sigh. "She is."

Obviously taking her agreement for encouragement, Cliff pressed on. "Do you know if she and Adam are—well, if they're—?"

With an impatient gesture, Haley set the mug of Irish coffee she'd been sipping down on the table with a loud thump. "No, Cliff, I don't know exactly what sort of relationship Adam and Sheila have at the moment, nor do I really care. If you do, I suggest that you ask her."

For the first time all evening, it finally seemed to dawn on Cliff that Haley was less than thrilled by his behavior. "You're not mad, are you?" he asked cautiously. "I mean, I know we've been seeing one another, but it isn't as if we have any sort of exclusive arrangement."

No, thought Haley, he was right about that. Although it was true that she had been dating Cliff exclusively, that fact was due more to circumstance than to the quality of the relationship that had developed between them. If she hadn't been so busy trying to convince herself that it would get better, she would have realized that she wasn't exactly thrilled with what they had. No kissing on the first date indeed! she thought, feeling perilously close to a hysterical giggle. And what had transpired since hadn't been any noticeable improvement, either!

Drawing several deep breaths, Haley felt herself growing calmer, and when she spoke again, her voice was remarkably even. "Mad?" she said coolly, raising one eyebrow. "Why on earth should I be mad? Just because my date took it into his head to humiliate me in public, I don't see any reason for getting all excited, do you?"

"Come on, Haley," Cliff said in his best barrister's tone, his voice low and soothing. "You know how I feel about you, but this is different. Sheila is different. Now you, you're the type of woman a man can have tremendous respect for—"

"Stop right there!" Haley cried, her sable eyes flashing dangerously, "because I feel it's only fair to warn you that if you try to tell me that you loved me for my mind, I'm going to punch you right in the nose!"

At that, Cliff's jaw dropped open, hung there for a moment, then snapped shut without his having uttered a word. They sat that way in silence for what seemed like decades, until the light trill of Sheila's laughter signaled that she and Adam were returning to the table.

"Ahem," said Adam, clearing his throat loudly at the sight of the suppressed hostility that greeted him. "Here are two people who look as though they could use some cheering up." Unlinking his arm from Sheila's, he pointed her in Cliff's direction and gave her a gentle nudge. "Why don't we switch partners and try the dance floor again? What do you say, Haley?" he asked, smiling down at her cheerfully. "Are you game?"

The last thing she needed right now was Adam's pity, Haley thought with a frown. Yet somehow, when he reached down to grasp her hand, she found herself allowing her fingers to be swallowed up by the warmth of his clasp; then, when he pulled out her chair, standing up as well; and finally, despite all intentions to the contrary, following him away toward the small dance floor.

He probably thought he was being subtle by asking her to dance, Haley decided crossly. But she knew what he was up to, all right. One look at her face back at the table must have told him that she was perilously close to an explosion, and knowing her temper as he did, he had acted accordingly by spiriting her quickly and quietly away. Now that the potential disaster had been averted, he probably meant to keep her away, occupying her time until her anger had had a chance to die down to a more manageable state. He was taking charge of her life again, she thought irritably. Who died and left him king, anyway?

All throughout the long first number, Haley remained defiantly silent. Her left hand resting lightly on Adam's shoulder, her right succumbing to his clasp but not in any way encouraging it; she held herself stiffly away, determined not to be lulled into a gentler frame of mind. As if he understood, Adam made no attempt at conversation, either, nor did he try to draw her any closer than she wished to be. Instead, he was content simply to guide her around the dance floor, the effortless grace of his movements meshing perfectly with the soft, soothing beat of the music.

One dance blended into two, and then three, as finally, without even really being aware of when the transformation had taken place, Haley began to relax. The hurt that had held her spine rigid slowly seeped away, replaced by a feeling of calm acceptance. It must be the liquor, she thought languidly, not demurring when Adam's arm encircled her waist with gentle possession and gathered her close. All those drinks she'd had that night were finally catching up with her—the two rounds before dinner, the bottle of wine with it, then the Irish coffee after—all consumed in a vain attempt to blunt the sharp stab of rejection she'd felt at Cliff's outrageous behavior. Not that she was drunk certainly, just pleasantly lightheaded, supremely relaxed and, here in Adam's arms, very, very content.

Soon, despite her intentions to the contrary, Haley found herself snuggled against the hard planes of Adam's chest, drinking in the pleasant, woodsy smell of his aftershave, which mingled with the even more pleasant aroma of Adam himself. Arching back into the hand that spanned her waist, she shuddered lightly as his fingers reached up to graze softly over the naked skin of her back, bared by the jump suit's halter design. A sudden shiver of delight winged its way up and down her spine; then the hand was reaching higher still, burrowing through the thick tresses of her hair to find the back of her neck and draw her closer with a gentle massage.

There was something terribly dangerous about what was happening, Haley thought dreamily. Adam was only doing his duty, after all. She'd been a friend in need, and for the second time that day, he'd felt obliged to come to her rescue. So, knowing all that to be true, why did she feel this treacherous delight in being wrapped within his arms, this deliciously pleasurable sensation at the delicate touch of his flesh against her own?

If she had any sense at all, she would be running hard and fast in the opposite direction, Haley decided. But at the moment, she was feeling anything but sensible. It had been a long day, one that had found her buffeted by a full range of conflicting emotions, and now, at its end, she was discovering that she simply hadn't the will to fight anymore. Here in Adam's arms, she felt safe and secure, as if nothing unpleasant could ever touch her again. Unconsciously, she sighed, a wistful, yearning sound that came from deep within her throat and escaped without warning. Adam's arms tightened around her then, molding her body to his own as he drew his head back and looked down at her searchingly.

"Are you ready to talk about it yet?" he asked.

"About what?" Haley asked innocently, knowing full well what he was referring to.

But Adam was not one given to humoring her and never had been. "About the topic which has had smoke coming out of your ears for the last twenty minutes or so," he growled. "Cliff, the wandering boy friend."

"No," Haley said firmly. "Quite frankly, I have nothing to say on that subject at all. But Sheila," she added, deftly turning the conversation away from herself, "now she's another topic entirely."

"Oh?" Adam cocked one eyebrow. "And just what do you have to say about her?"

Plenty of things, Haley thought crossly, but I'm too big a person to mention most of them. Straightening, she pulled herself fractionally away. "I really don't see why you're going out with her," she commented, making a concerted effort to be fair. "It's obvious that she can't keep up with you at all."

Looking down at her, Adam grinned devilishly. "Oh, I don't know," he drawled. "I think she does quite well. Actually, her drives won't even peak for another couple of years, whereas if I'm to believe what I read, I'm on the down slide already."

"That's not what I meant, and you know it!" Haley grumbled into his shirt front.

"Look at me, Haley," Adam ordered softly. Releasing her right hand, he laid it against his chest, trapping it between them as he reached down to place the tip of his forefinger beneath her chin and tilt her face upward to his. "Are you upset about what happened tonight? Does Cliff really mean that much to you?"

For a brief moment, Haley thought before answering. "No," she admitted finally, knowing that her pride was wounded more than anything else. "But that doesn't mean I've been having the time of my life. Believe me, it's no picnic watching when a woman with the mental capabilities of a turnip and a physical endowment the size of Texas has both men at the table treating her like visiting royalty."

"What's the matter?" Adam grinned. "Are you jealous of Sheila's womanly charms?"

"Not in the slightest," Haley sniffed, quickly crossing two fingers on the hand that lay atop Adam's shoulder. "Why would I want to be built like that? Why, the poor woman looks like she's wearing a life jacket that's been permanently overinflated."

"You're being catty," said Adam, leaning down to whisper the words in her ear, his face hovering so close to hers that she could feel the warm, even fan of his breath against her hair, "and it doesn't become you. As a point of fact, those weren't the womanly charms I was referring to at all."

"Oh?" Haley snapped, pulling her head deliberately away.

"Sheila is a very feminine woman, and I don't mean that in just the physical sense. She's soft and gentle, and she's not afraid to be vulnerable. There's a wonderful supportive quality about her. She may not talk much, but she's an excellent listener."

"The very traits which attracted Cliff right to her, I'm sure," Haley shot back sarcastically. "Why, I'll bet as we entered the dining room tonight, he took one look at Sheila and said to himself, 'That woman looks like a wonderful listener to me.'"

At that, Adam laughed out loud, a rich melodic sound that Haley not only heard but also felt, the fingers that rested lightly against his chest pulsating with the deep, rumbling vibration. "You may have a point there," he conceded.

"Well, if you liked that point," she said affably, "here's another. In case you haven't noticed, I'm not the only one who got left high and dry this evening. Cliff may have been all over Sheila, but I didn't exactly see her trying to push him away."

"That's true," Adam said slowly, his gray eyes seeking out hers and holding them, "but I'm afraid I have a bit of a confession to make. Sheila and I had already decided before tonight that our relationship wasn't working out the way we wanted it to. Our date this evening was really just sort of one last time for the road. Actually, that's the reason I was so quick to ask her to dance. I wanted to get her alone so I could tell her that if she wanted to leave with Cliff, it was all right with me. In fact, I doubt very much that they'll both still be there when we get back to the table."

For a moment, Haley was utterly incredulous, her mind unable to comprehend what she had heard. "I can't believe you would do such a thing!" she cried, outraged. Bracing both hands against his chest, she shoved him away forcibly. "Do you mean to tell me that you had the nerve to send my date home with another woman without even doing me the courtesy of consulting me first?"

Gathering her back into his arms, Adam ignored her struggle of protest and the angry frown that went with it as he began to move them in time to the music once more. "It seemed like a good idea at the time," he said carefully. "From the way you've been shooting daggers at Cliff all evening, I didn't exactly get the impression you were thrilled with his company."

She couldn't argue with that logic, Haley decided, and instead remained silent.

"Come on, cheer up," Adam said soothingly. "You've already admitted that the guy didn't mean anything to you, so why the long face now? Maybe we should be happy that they've found one another. After all, who are we to stand in the way of true love?"

"True lust, you mean," Haley muttered, but she was fast discovering that cradled close against the strong, comforting wall of Adam's chest as she was, it was difficult to stay angry at anything, much less him, for very long. Drawing back her head, she grinned up at him reluctantly. "I'll say one thing for you," she mused aloud. "You certainly don't make a very possessive lover."

"No, you're right," Adam agreed solemnly. "I've always felt that jealousy is a destructive emotion, with no place at all in a good, solid relationship. As far as I'm concerned, the only good reason for two people to be together is because that's where they both want to be. Otherwise, you're much better off breaking things up amiably and parting as friends."

Resting her head against the broad expanse of Adam's chest, Haley slid her arms upward from his shoulders to wind them around his neck, her fingers tangling in the soft, curling wisps of hair at his nape. "Sweet, amiable Adam," she murmured dreamily, the cumulative effect of his continued nearness beginning to act as a potent drug to her receptive senses. "If you make a habit of breaking up with all your women so nicely, you must have quite a large collection of friends."

"No," Adam said softly, relaxing against her to bury his face in her hair. Slowly, Haley became aware of the light, delicate touch of his lips brushing over the top of her head in a feathery caress. "That's a spot I reserve for only certain, very special people."

Tilting back her head, Haley looked up, her dark eyes open wide with wonder at the tenderness of his tone. Their gazes met, then locked, fusing in a shock of elemental communication that needed no words at all to convey its meaning.

He was going to kiss her, Haley realized suddenly. He wanted to kiss her, and not only that, she wanted him to. She wanted to feel the hard imprint of his lips on her own, to explore the secret depths of his mouth with her tongue, to surrender herself fully to the power of his embrace. Unwittingly, she moistened her half-parted lips, drawing the tip of her tongue slowly over their soft outline, her invitation unconscious but clear nonetheless as she felt herself engulfed by a tide of sensation whose desire was as strong as it was inevitable.

For a brief moment, time seemed suspended between them. Neither moved or scarcely dared to breathe as the sensual electricity that sparked between them seemed to fill the air. Then, almost as if by sheer force of will, Adam was pulling away, and the message conveyed in the depths of his smoldering gray eyes was gone, replaced instead by an emotion that she could not name at all. The moment of heightened awareness that vibrated between them had passed. Regretfully, Haley watched it go.

Briskly, Adam's hands slipped across her shoulders to the tops of her arms as he straightened and set her away. "Time to leave," he muttered, his voice sounding curiously hoarse. Without waiting for her assent, he grasped her hand and led her from the dance floor.

It took only a moment for them to retrieve their things from the table; then they were outside in the warm, heavy night air, and Adam was handing over his ticket stub to the valet and receiving the keys to the Zee. Once inside the low-slung car, he seemed determined not to succumb to the mood of intimacy prompted by its small interior. He talked nonstop as he drove, his conversation light, impersonal and not at all deterred by the occasional grunts that were all Haley could seem to muster in response.

Settling back into the deep bucket seat, she closed her eyes and let her thoughts drift. As far as Adam was concerned, that brief, magical interlude on the dance floor might never even have happened. He was certainly taking pains to make that clear. And that was too bad, Haley mused dreamily, for she was still caught up in the heady power of its spell and not at all sure that she wanted it to end.

Reaching the cottage, Adam parked beside the Rabbit and walked her to the door, but he made no move to follow her inside.

"Wouldn't you like to come in?" Haley invited, her mind floating, still floating.

"I don't think so," Adam replied, and once again she was struck by the curiously gruff quality of his tone. "Not tonight."

He started back toward the car, and of their own volition, Haley's eyes followed him. Unexpectedly, she was shocked by the sense of loss she felt at his departure.

"Adam?" she called after him, her voice soft, tremulous.

Pausing on the walk, he turned to her and waited silently.

"Thank you for the dance," she whispered, her voice carried to him by the slight breeze.

To her surprise, Adam flashed her a crooked grin. "Anytime, kid," he replied jauntily, then turned and continued on his way.

Abruptly, Haley stiffened, his unexpected use of the old nickname bringing her up short with all the efficacy of a bucket of cold water dashed directly into her face. Kid? she repeated silently to herself, scowling at his departing back. *Kid?*

Stepping back, Haley closed the door between them with a loud thud, her lips compressed in a small, perplexed frown. Oh, well, she thought, sighing. So much for romance. It was back to business as usual.

4

Haley had all day Sunday to think about the foolish way she'd behaved the night before, and she used the time to full advantage.

Was it really only the previous day that she'd resolved not to let Adam get to her again? she mused, lounging on her terrace in the sun. That was one resolution that must have set the record for brevity! Good going, Morgan, she thought, shaking her head contemptuously. Great self-control. Talk about blatant! The night before, she'd done everything but throw herself at Adam's feet, crying, "Take me, I'm yours."

"Blah!" Haley stuck out her tongue in a deprecating gesture of disgust. The only saving grace to the whole episode was that Adam couldn't possibly have known what was really on her mind. And if it ever came up again, she intended to lie shamelessly. So she'd invited him in. Big deal! For all he knew, she could have been offering anything—a nightcap, a cup of coffee, an impromptu writing session . . .

Abruptly, Haley frowned. Just what *had* she been offering, anyway? For a brief moment, she pondered that thought, then thrust it aside, realizing that it had no ready answer. She honestly didn't know what would have happened between them if Adam had accepted her invitation and followed her inside. Nor did she know what she wanted to have happen. Not that it really mattered, anyway, for things had never had a chance to progress that far. Adam had wasted no time at all in reminding her of the parameters of their relationship. Kid indeed! Of all the nerve! Did she go around making derogatory comments about his age? Of course not. Maybe she ought to try calling him gramps once or twice and see how he liked that!

The small giggle that followed that thought left Haley feeling much better. Besides, she decided, she may have played a part in what had happened, but it wasn't as if the whole fiasco had been *all* her fault. No, that look Adam had given her on the dance floor had been very real. For a moment, however brief, his thoughts had mirrored hers exactly; she was sure of it! After all, Adam was the one with the vivid imagination, not she!

No, Haley concluded with a sigh, she was the rational partner—the sane, careful, logical one. And now the only logical thing to do was to accept the obvious—no matter what Adam might have felt while she was dancing in his arms, it was not something he had wanted to pursue. The only rational response to that was to act in kind—to simply put the whole episode behind her and go on about life as if nothing had happened.

Early Monday morning, Adam arrived at the cottage with a box of doughnuts under his arm and a broad grin on his face, exuding all the breezy charm of a man who hadn't a care in the world. Haley needed no prompting to match his cheery mood.

"You look like a man who got up on the right side of bed this morning," she said, leading the way into the kitchen where she poured them each a tall glass of milk.

"Of course," Adam declared. A broad, sweeping gesture of his arm encompassed the whole room. "A box of doughnuts, a glass of milk and thou—what more could any man ask?"

Shaking her head at his mangled version of the quotation, Haley laughed in spite of herself. "Don't you think that's going a bit heavy on the poetic license?"

Blithely, Adam shrugged. "This morning, I feel poetic. We're on the verge of creating the great American novel. I can feel it in my bones." Walking into the alcove, he set the doughnuts down on the table between the two typewriters, then sat down in his chair. "Come on," he invited, ogling her teasingly. "What do you say you and I get romantic?"

To their mutual delight, it turned out to be one of those rare occasions when everything went perfectly. Their writing was fast and fluid, and page after page of flowing prose piled up on the table between them. By turns, they composed in silence by themselves, then aloud in boisterous cooperation as their enthusiasm for the scenes overtook them and each raced to supply the perfect quip, the best description, the snippet of dialogue that would make their characters come alive.

"What do you think of this?" asked Adam. They had reached the point midway through the book where Rex and Allegra would share their first love scene—an important undertaking and one they both wanted to get just right. "Imagine that he's come to her hotel room unexpectedly. He knocks, but there's no answer. Then he tries the door and realizes that it isn't locked. That upsets him—he's beginning to feel quite strongly about Allegra, remember, and he pushes the door open and storms into the room just as she emerges from the bathroom, wearing nothing but a towel wrapped around her naked body."

"I'm with you so far," said Haley, typing away furiously as he spoke. "Then what?"

" 'Rex looked her up and down from the tops of her golden blonde hair to the tips of her dainty feet,' " Adam dictated. " 'Then he said in a hushed tone of voice, "I want you, Allegra." ' "

"Hmmm," said Haley, looking down at the lines she had typed. She picked up her pen from the table and began to chew on its end thoughtfully. "That's not bad except for the last part. 'I want you, Allegra.' Don't you think that's a little abrupt?"

"Believe me," Adam said wolfishly, "in that situation, that's exactly what any red-blooded male would be thinking."

"Maybe." Haley frowned. "But that doesn't mean he has to blurt out exactly what's on his mind. I'd much rather see him try a little romantic persuasion first. You know, whispering sweet nothings and all that? We want to set the right mood, after all. Allegra should be wooed, courted, seduced—not just tossed down on the bed and taken."

"Oh, I don't know." Adam chuckled, his gray eyes glinting mischievously. "That idea has its merits."

"And you sir, have a one-track mind," Haley scoffed. "You're just lucky you've got me around to clean up your act for you. Now picture this. Rex walks into the room, looks at Allegra and says, 'You are a vision of loveliness. You look like a goddess, all pale and golden. You are Botticelli's *Venus*, Raphael's *Madonna*, Picasso's *Dancer*—'"

"Picasso's *Dancer* had three breasts and one eye," Adam pointed out mildly.

"All right, strike that," said Haley. Grabbing the pen that was clutched between her lips, she scribbled over the paper. "'You look like a goddess, all pale and golden,'" she repeated thoughtfully, replacing the pen in her mouth as she began to type once more. "'I want to worship your body.'"

"'I want to kiss your sweet lips,'" Adam contributed from the other end of the table.

"'I'm going half out of my mind from wanting you!'" Haley cried enthusiastically, delighted by her addition.

"You're turning blue," Adam remarked, glancing up at her over the tops of the two machines.

Haley, still caught up in the dramatic moment, nodded absently and continued to type, adding his words to what they had already written. Then, abruptly, her fingers stilled on the keys. She frowned and read the last few lines aloud, "'I want to kiss your sweet lips. I'm going half out of my mind from wanting you. *You're turning blue'?*" Looking up, she stared at Adam skeptically. "I don't know about you, but that's hardly my idea of sweet nothings."

"Not Allegra." Adam grinned. "You. You're turning blue. Your pen is leaking ink. All over your lips, to be exact."

"Oh, nuts!" cried Haley, spitting out the offending ballpoint. She reached up and rubbed the back of her hand back and forth across her mouth. "There, is that better?"

Adam peered at her from across the table. "Actually, it's worse," he announced, showing no sympathy at all. "Now you've smeared it."

Haley glared at him stonily.

"Hold on, I'll fix it for you." Adam jumped up and disappeared into the kitchen, reappearing several moments later with a wet towel. Bending over her solicitously, he placed one finger under her chin and tilted her face up to his. Immediately, Haley became aware of the nearness of his lips, hovering only inches above her own. Involuntarily, her dark eyes fixed there, drawn to the firm, sensuous curve of his mouth, which, as she watched, broke into a wide grin.

"Now what's so funny?" she muttered irritably, tearing her eyes away.

Adam positioned the towel just above her face but made no effort to get on with the chore. "Actually, you look kind of cute with blue lips," he commented. "Rather like the bride of Dracula must have looked when he got through with her, I imagine."

"Very amusing," Haley snapped, increasingly unnerved by his presence so close at hand. Deliberately, she drew a deep, calming breath, only to have her senses teased by the heady masculine scent that surrounded him. "Now if you're through laughing at my expense, do you mind getting on with the cleanup?"

To his credit, Adam did. And if Haley spent the next several minutes in a turmoil of delightful sensations, savoring the gentle touch of his fingers as he cleaned the soft, sensitive skin of her lips, she had only herself to blame. Adam, for his part, was all efficiency, the only incongruous note being the silly, self-satisfied smile that creased his face as he cupped her chin with his large hand and gently dabbed at her mouth with the moist towel.

It was almost as if he were privy to a private joke that she herself was not aware of, Haley decided, looking up at him. Because she saw nothing funny about the situation at all. Nerve-racking, aggravating and embarrassing, maybe, but funny? Never!

"There you go, all done," Adam said finally, stepping back to admire his handiwork. "Good as new."

"Thank you," Haley mumbled rudely.

Though she felt his eyes on her, she turned her attention deliberately away, concentrating instead on the piece of paper still rolled through her typewriter. She knew that her lips were reddened and slightly swollen from his ministrations, tingling in a way that was not at all unpleasant; and she couldn't help but feel that for all his apparent nonchalance, there had been an underlying sensuality in the way Adam's hands had held and cleaned her face. Indeed, she suspected that nothing else he might have done could have left her feeling any more aware of him than she was at that moment.

That, however, was her own business, for she was damned if she'd give him the satisfaction of knowing he'd gotten to her again. She'd let herself respond to him the other night, and look where that had gotten her. The very last thing she wanted right now was for him to start teasing her again!

"Okay, let's get on with it," she said with a cheeriness that sounded somewhat forced. She lifted up the sheet of typing paper and read the last few lines aloud. " 'I want to kiss your sweet lips. I'm going half out of my mind from wanting you' sounds good to me. Do you want to go with that?"

"Anytime you're ready," Adam drawled meaningfully.

Abruptly, Haley glanced up in surprise. While she'd been reading, he had sat down on the corner of the table next to her machine, and now he was gazing down at her, his expression thoughtful. He looked, Haley decided, as if teasing her was the last thing on his mind. But still . . .

"Be serious, would you!" She laughed, swatting playfully at his rear end. Using both hands, she braced herself against the side of his hip and pushed until he toppled off the table's edge and landed on his feet. "Go on. Get back down to your own seat. How do you ever expect to get any work done?"

"All right," Adam grumbled good-naturedly. "You don't have to get pushy. I'm going."

Back in his chair, he began to compose aloud once more. " 'Quickly, impatiently, Rex strode across the room. Allegra's eyes widened like those of a frightened doe as she watched him come. Then he grasped her naked shoulders and pulled her into his arms. She began to struggle furiously—' "

"Hold it right there!" Haley cried, making no attempt to hide her outrage. " 'She began to struggle furiously'? You've got to be kidding me!"

"What's the matter with that?" Adam asked calmly. "That's the way these things always go. Besides, how else are we going to get the towel to fall off?"

"Who said anything about the towel falling off?" Haley demanded. "They haven't even kissed yet, and already you've got her standing around naked. Talk about male chauvinism! Suppose we took off all of Rex's clothes. How would you feel about that?"

"Haley," Adam said slowly, the merest hint of a smile playing about his lips. "Did it ever occur to you that you're taking all of this a bit—well, personally?"

"Don't try to change the subject! This has nothing at all to do with me. It's the honor and dignity of all womanhood that's at stake here."

"All womanhood, hmm?" said Adam, pursing his lips reflectively. "Well, then, speaking for all mankind, I'm sure nobody would object if you insist on making Rex stark naked as well, although how you're going to explain how he managed to get through the hotel lobby to her room in that condition is beyond me."

Shaking her head, Haley dissolved in helpless laughter. "You know," she said, peering at him closely, "if I didn't know you better, I'd say that you had latent exhibitionist tendencies."

"Who, me?" Adam said innocently.

Pointedly, Haley ignored him. "I still don't like the idea of her struggling with him," she mused aloud. "If Allegra doesn't want to be kissed, then she shouldn't have to be."

"I, for one, don't care what Allegra wants," Adam declared. "We've reached the point in the book where it's time to expand their relationship into a more physical realm."

"Fine," Haley conceded. "I agree with you totally on that point. But why do they have to fight about it? Why can't we make Allegra every bit as willing as Rex is?"

"Because it will read better this way. Besides, don't forget about the towel falling off."

"Oh, hang the towel!" Haley snapped in exasperation. "If you don't stop harping about that, I'm going to put her in a bathrobe instead—a big, thick, fuzzy one made out of flaming orange chenille with a high neck and long sleeves!"

"Okay, okay." Adam laughed. "For the time being, we'll forget the towel."

"And the struggle," Haley added quickly. "I have no desire to write a book where women go around being seduced when they don't want to be."

"Why not?" asked Adam, sounding truly curious.

"Well, because!" Haley sputtered, wondering how he could overlook something so patently obvious. "For one thing, it isn't realistic."

"Sure it is," Adam said with a wolfish grin. "And not only that, it's titillating as hell."

"I still don't buy it," Haley insisted stubbornly. "I'm tired of reading books where the heroine gets kissed whether she wants to or not. For Pete's sake, why don't they just break free? I mean, I know men are stronger and all, but—"

"But nothing," said Adam, crossing his arms over his chest complacently. "If I had my arms around you and I didn't want to let go, there is no way you could get away from me."

"You think so, do you?" Haley cocked one eyebrow upward.

"I'm sure of it."

That was one challenge Haley wasn't going to let slide by. If there was one thing Adam Burke needed desperately, it was a large dent in his overinflated sense of male superiority!

"All right." She grinned, standing up. "Bring your steel bands over here, and let's give it a go!"

"You got it."

Adam rose from his chair and strode purposefully into the living room, Haley trailing along in his wake. He stopped in the middle of the large cream-colored carpet that covered the center of the floor, braced his feet several inches apart and beckoned her to him with a knowing grin.

"Why is it that I feel like Daniel about to enter the lion's den?" Haley muttered under her breath as she crossed the room to stand before him.

Uncertainly, she reached out to place her hands lightly on the tops of his shoulders, careful to keep almost a full foot of space between them. Adam, however, was having none of it. Ignoring her reticence, he wound both arms tightly around her waist and drew her to him. Instinct prompted her to brace back slightly, testing the waters before plunging in, but the implacable strength that met her slight resistance was more than enough to give her second thoughts about the validity of her own theory.

"Well," Adam prompted, "what are you waiting for?"

"I just wanted to make sure you were ready," said Haley, hoping that her voice conveyed more confidence than she felt. All of a sudden, she was sure it was not one of her better ideas.

"Anytime you are," Adam replied cheerfully. Looking down, he flashed her a cheeky grin. "You know, kid, I think I'm going to like doing research with you."

At that, Haley's head snapped up in surprise. That name again! Now what was Adam up to?

There was no time to ponder the thought, however, for Haley was quickly discovering that at the moment she had other, far more pressing matters to worry about. Once more, her traitorous senses were coming alive with the tingling heat of sexual awareness as their bodies molded together like two interlocking pieces of the same puzzle. They stood hip to hip and thigh to thigh, and she was achingly conscious of the compelling, virile strength of the man whose body surrounded her own. Though she held herself away as far as Adam's arms would permit, it was not enough. The tips of her breasts, unconfined beneath her loose peasant-style blouse, brushed lightly against the sinewed muscles of his chest in an inadvertent caress that left her nipples taut with reaction. The smooth skin of her legs was tickled by the crisp sprinkling of hairs that covered his, and Haley felt as though all her nerve endings had been sensitized, honed to fever pitch by the contact.

Then, with an angry toss of her head, Haley banished those thoughts. Perversely, her attraction heightened rather than diminished her determination to break free, and she readied herself mentally for what was to come. "Okay," she announced, "here I go."

That was her first mistake, Haley decided a moment later, for no sooner had she declared her intentions than Adam had braced himself for the struggles to follow. Gritting her teeth in helpless frustration, she pushed and pulled against him with all her might, only to find that he held her easily in place, seemingly with no more exertion than he might have used to read the morning paper. Why on earth had she been so stupid as to announce she was ready? Haley castigated herself. Didn't she know that the element of surprise was crucial at times like this?

"See?" Adam taunted her, and she could cheerfully have slapped the mocking smile from his face. "I told you you couldn't get away."

"Oh, yeah, macho man?" Haley muttered, dismayed to realize that her breath was coming in short, shallow puffs, a condition that she quickly attributed to the exertion rather than to the proximity of a strong, hard male body. "Well, we'll just see about that."

Sheer stubbornness prompted her to redouble her efforts. She may have sensed that it was a losing battle, but Haley had no intention of admitting defeat without at least putting up one hell of a good fight! Adam might win this round, but before she was through with him, he would realize that containing a woman who was struggling furiously could give a man more urgent things to think about than the possibility of a few stolen kisses!

Cursing eloquently under her breath, Haley swung her weight first to the right and then to the left, hoping to shift Adam's guard and catch him off balance. For several minutes, she struggled in vain; then, finally, the opening she was looking for presented itself when she felt Adam loosen one of the arms that were locked about her waist, sliding his hand upward as he sought a better hold. Immediately, she braced her feet, then shoved him away with all her might. As she'd expected, he countered the move with one of his own, shifting one foot back several inches to redistribute his weight and consolidate his position.

At that, Haley permitted herself a small, self-satisfied grin. So far, so good. Quickly, before there was time for him to realize what she had in mind, she slid her leg into the opening between his two, intending to wrap her foot around the back of his calf and jerk it forward, a move she'd seen demonstrated once in a women's self-defense class and one that, if properly executed, should send him sprawling down onto the floor in an undignified heap.

But if Haley's reflexes were fast, Adam's were even more so. No sooner had she started her move than he was bringing his leg forward once more. In a moment, Haley realized, she would be trapped, more helpless than before! Even knowing that she had lost the element of surprise, she forged ahead, anyway. To her dismay, however, the quick, thrusting jerk of her foot was knocked aside by his forward motion, and the maneuver, which should have been lateral, snapped upward instead.

As soon as she'd made contact, Haley realized with a sick feeling in the pit of her stomach that her mother had been right about the defensive properties of knees when applied to the appropriate portions of the male anatomy. With a strangled groan, Adam released her, then slipped down onto the floor at her feet, rolling from side to side and moaning loudly.

"Oh, my God, I'm so sorry!" Haley cried in horror, kneeling down beside him. "Are you all right? Oh, Adam, I never meant to—"

The apology, however, was never completed, for as she reached out tentatively with one hand to touch Adam's shoulder and turn him to her, he rolled quickly to one side, his hand snaking out to grasp hers and pull her down onto the floor.

"Oh!" she gasped, surprise and the jarring effect of the fall combining to leave her quite breathless.

In a single fluid motion, Adam rose to one knee and straddled her body, lowering himself carefully down onto her stomach as his hands captured each of her wrists in turn and held them captive on either side of her head. Trapped beneath him, Haley glowered upward. Belatedly, she realized that judging from Adam's sudden recovery, he must have succeeded in deflecting her blow. The whole ploy had been nothing but a feint, a ruse designed to throw her off guard and capture her sympathy. And she, dope that she was, had fallen for his act hook, line and sinker!

"You louse!" she cried, laughing in relief. "You absolute stinker! And to think I was afraid I'd actually hurt you!"

Looking down at her, Adam winked lasciviously. "Man's strongest instinct," he assured her solemnly, "is to ensure the propagation of the species."

"Even at *your* age?" Haley inquired sweetly.

"You may live to regret those words," Adam drawled, settling himself down more firmly over her hips.

All at once, Haley was very much aware of the vulnerability of her position. "Adam Burke, you let me up this instant!" she demanded with as much bravado as she could muster under the circumstances.

"Not until you admit you were wrong," Adam said silkily, ignoring her struggles as she squirmed helplessly beneath him. "Admit it, Haley. The male is a physically superior animal."

"Are you sure you wouldn't like to beat your chest for emphasis?" Haley said dryly.

"Say it."

"Can't talk anymore," Haley groaned, trying a ploy of her own. "Adam, you're crushing me. You're too heavy."

"Nonsense." Adam grinned. "I'm resting most of my weight on my knees, not your hips. Sorry, kid, but that one won't fly."

"Don't call me that!" Haley snapped, suddenly annoyed by the whole turn of events.

Once again, Adam's timing was nothing short of abominable! With him sitting on top of her as he was, his position achingly similar to that of a far more intimate endeavor, Haley was supremely aware of her own femininity and the womanly needs that he aroused deep within her body. Didn't he realize, at that particular moment, that there was nothing remotely childlike about the way she was feeling?

"Why not?" Adam asked curiously. Releasing her hands, he scooted back several inches, then rocked back so that Haley was able to pull herself up into a sitting position, although her thighs still lay trapped between the implacable strength of his. "I myself happen to think that it's a particularly appropriate nickname for an old friend, one that I have known since she was little more than a child."

"Oh, please, I was twenty years old when we first met," Haley groaned in protest. Her arms propped straight out behind her, she leaned back onto her palms, trying valiantly to ignore the fact that her face was now at eye level with the hard, corded muscles of his chest. "I know it isn't often that you manage to get the upper hand, but just because you seem to have finally come out on top for once, is that any reason to rub it in by insulting me?"

"Insulting you?" Adam raised one eyebrow in disbelief. "Is that what you think I'm doing?"

Silently, Haley nodded.

"Believe me," said Adam, "my calling you kid is not in any way meant to be demeaning. Quite the contrary, in fact. I see it as a sign of my affection, much like all those trite, hackneyed words that everybody else seems to use—darling, sweetheart, honey." He frowned in disapproval. "They're so clichéd, don't you think?"

Haley opened her mouth to disagree, but before there was time to speak, Adam had continued on. "But kid, now there's a name with a tradition and a history. It has its own private meaning that immediately brings to mind how truly special our friendship is."

How truly special, Haley's thoughts echoed softly. Put like that, she had to admit that being referred to as kid didn't seem half bad at all. Especially not now when Adam continued to kneel with his body wrapped around hers, his hands, with their long, strong fingers, resting on his knees, his face only inches from her own.

Could he really be so unaware of the devastating effect he was having on her senses? Haley wondered, feeling the tension begin to coil through her body like a tightly wound spring. The urge to lower herself back down to the floor, to grasp Adam's shoulders and pull him down on top of her, was overwhelming. The question was Did she dare?

"My writer's soul shudders at such lack of originality," Adam was saying and, thoroughly incredulous, Haley realized that he was still discussing semantics. "But I guess if that's what you want, I can give it a try. Now, which shall it be?"

Her dark eyes opened wide, and she stared at him in utter consternation.

Seeing her confusion, Adam held up one hand and began to tick off the choices on his fingers. "Darling?" Catching Haley's eye, he grimaced expressively. "Baby?" The face he made this time was even worse. "How about Sugar?" Frowning, he stuck out his tongue in distaste.

"Okay, okay, I get the picture." Haley laughed nervously as she strove to marshal her composure and regain some sense of normalcy in this decidedly odd situation. "I take back what I said. Kid will be just fine."

Quite without her conscious consent, her hips writhed back and forth suddenly between his thighs, twisting, straining for his touch. Good Lord! Haley thought, clamping the muscles back under control. This wouldn't do at all. She needed something, anything, to take her mind off him!

Smiling deliberately, she affected a light, breezy tone. "So tell me, since you're the one who's all for unusual names, just what would you like me to call you?"

"Let me see," said Adam. He fluttered his eyelashes modestly. "How about Your Highness?"

"Fat chance," Haley scoffed, grinning at him wickedly. All at once she knew exactly how she was going to get even with him for this nefarious assault on her body. "How about Chuckles?"

That was all the warning he got of her intentions, and it wasn't enough. Her hands snaked out and grasped him about the waist, her long, slender fingers finding the ticklish spot just below his ribs and attacking it mercilessly.

"What the hell—!" Adam swore, leaping back in reaction as he twisted to evade her. Then, with a soft growl, he was upon her as well, his strong fingers immediately seeking out the vulnerable parts of her body as Haley fell back with a shriek.

"Don't!" she squealed, rolling across the floor as he came after her. "Adam, no—!"

Gasping with laughter, they wrestled about on the rug like two children at play, their enthusiasm for the game gleeful and unrestrained. The vigorous physical release was just what Haley needed, and she plunged into the play with reckless abandon, heedless of the fact that between Adam's longer arms and stronger grasp, she didn't stand a chance. Giggling helplessly before the onslaught, she refused to give in, her hands roaming over his body with careless familiarity as each one strove to gain the advantage.

It was several minutes before Adam succeeded in pinning her once more. This time, he took no chances, covering the entire length of her body with his own. Breathless with laughter, flushed with exertion, Haley gazed up at her captor, prepared to concede her defeat. Instead, she discovered that his face was startlingly near, his gray eyes smoldering with a passionate intent that made her breath catch in her throat and her heartbeat quicken in her breast, driving all other thought from her mind.

For a brief moment, they simply stared at one another in meaningful silence, their faces so near that Haley felt his breath like a warm caress upon her cheek. Then, still without speaking, Adam shifted his weight slightly, and she understood that she was free to move away if she wished.

She didn't.

"I'm going to kiss you, Haley," Adam said softly, his voice no more than a throaty whisper.

"Yes," Haley whispered, granting permission and at the same time affirming her own desires.

Cradling her in his arms, Adam came to her slowly. Their mouths met and moved together in sweet harmony, his kiss everything Haley had always known it would be—gentle, tender, yet infinitely persuasive. She shuddered beneath the impact of his touch as the feelings she had denied for so long surged to the fore, not abandoned as she had thought but merely suppressed and now ready to reassert themselves once more. Her lips parted slightly, urging him closer, an invitation Adam gladly accepted until it seemed as though the tongue that probed the soft recesses of her mouth had access to the deep inner reaches of her soul as well.

All at once, Haley felt deliciously lightheaded, grateful for the floor that lay beneath her, for at that moment, she was sure she could not have supported herself. Her hands reached up tentatively to find his face and frame it, her palms lying flat along the angled curve of his jaw as she held him close.

It was right between them, Haley thought dazedly. So very right. She could feel it. Yet somewhere deep inside, the lingering doubts still persisted. Who were they really? she wondered. Rex and Allegra or Adam and Haley? Two characters playing out a scene to its logical conclusion or two friends unleashing desires that had been held in check for far too long? How would she ever know the truth?

"Adam?" she murmured huskily, not quite sure whether she uttered his name in protest or supplication.

His lips trailed a series of soft, feathery kisses across her cheek, then down the slope of her jaw before his tongue found the smooth shell of her ear. Grasping the lobe gently between his teeth, he pulled it into his mouth and sucked on it deeply. Haley moaned, twisting helplessly beneath him, ensnared in the passionate spell he was weaving around them.

Hang Allegra for getting in the way! she thought irreverently. What she felt there in Adam's arms was real, very real. This man was hers. This moment was hers. And she intended to make the most of it!

Caught up in her thoughts, it was a moment before Haley realized that the hand that had held her waist was moving inexorably upward, sliding over the gauzy shirt up past her ribs to settle just below the rounded swell of her breast. There it stopped, and the heat of the four fingers splayed against her side seemed to burn into the smooth muscles of her back as Adam's thumb began to move in a lazy caress, brushing back and forth over the bottom curve of the sensitive mound. Immediately, the nipple stiffened in response, jutting upward and clearly visible through the thin material of her blouse. Adam's answering growl was a sound of pure male satisfaction, and it was that which brought Haley back to her senses at last.

"Adam," she said once more, her voice stronger this time, more sure.

The hand that till now had been content to tease the perimeter slid silkily upward to claim full possession.

"Aaa-dam!" Haley gasped breathlessly, thoroughly unnerved by the searing shaft of fire that coursed suddenly through her veins. Her dark eyes opened wide as she tried unsuccessfully to twist away. "What are you doing?"

"Research," Adam murmured throatily. Ignoring her protest, he took full advantage of his new position, cupping her breast gently in his large hand, squeezing and molding the soft flesh as his thumb caressed the hard, tingling tip.

"Like hell you are!" Haley snapped, but a thread of reluctant amusement laced through her tone.

Oh, God, she just wasn't sure! Was this really meant to be, or was it all a mistake? Was it the blossoming of another facet in their relationship or simply two sets of hormones raging out of control and nothing more?

Another kiss, Haley mused. That was what was needed here. It was really the only logical solution. Another kiss to help her decide.

Reaching upward, she burrowed her fingers into Adam's thick mahogany-brown hair, holding his head steady as their mouths sought each other once more. This time, however, there was a difference. Gone was the tenderness he had shown before, replaced instead by a persuasive mastery that bespoke his growing need, and all at once the time for thought was past. Haley felt herself being swept along by the fire he had sparked between them, and when his hands slid back down along her body to her hips, she arched upward mindlessly, delighting in the feel of his hard weight pressing her down into the soft rug and crushing her resistance.

He parted her lips with his tongue, slipping inside to taste and sample the sweetness within, and Haley found herself responding to him feverishly, recklessly, with no thought at all to the future or past or to anything save the sensuous pleasure she derived from his touch and the compellingly fierce tide of sensation that rose up and overwhelmed her meager defenses.

It was the kiss she had imagined in her dreams, lived in her fantasies, longed for in her soul. And now that it was there, the reality far outshone anything she might have imagined. Seven years she had waited, Haley mused dreamily, and it was worth every minute.

5

She was trembling all over when Adam finally released her. Slowly, reluctantly, he pulled away. Cupping her face in the palms of his hands, he gazed down on her as she lay helplessly beneath him, powerless to move, powerless to think, lucky she was even able to breathe, so devastating was the effect the kiss had had on her senses.

They had always been honest with one another, and now, as she drew in a deep, calming breath, Haley could only say in wonder, "Where on earth did you ever learn to kiss like that?"

Above her, Adam smiled, and she realized suddenly from the stunned, faraway look in his eyes that she was not the only one who'd been swamped by reaction. Absently, he reached down with one hand to smooth back the silky black locks that had fallen across her forehead. "I was about to ask you the same thing," he murmured softly.

Now what? wondered Haley, trying valiantly to marshal her addled thoughts back into some semblance of order. Play it cool, an inner voice told her. Keep things light. Pretend that it was all a game, because as far as Adam's concerned, that's probably all it was.

"Well," she said brightly, easing herself out from beneath him. "I guess I'll have to take back all those mean things I thought about Sheila, because if that's any sample of the results, your flower child must be some teacher."

Adam, to his credit, saw her attempt at lightness and matched it. "On the contrary," he drawled, rising fluidly to his feet, then extending a hand downward to help her up as well. "It was a blonde, blue-eyed siren named Melissa who was responsible for teaching me everything I know."

"Melissa?" Haley frowned, quickly searching through her memory. "That's funny. I don't remember her at all."

"You wouldn't." Adam chuckled. "I'm afraid she was a little before your time." Pausing, he stroked his chin thoughtfully. "Actually, as I recall, I was eight, and she a bewitching, beguiling older woman of nine."

"Good Lord." Haley laughed in spite of herself. "You did believe in starting young, didn't you?"

"Well, you know what they say," Adam said modestly. "Practice makes perfect."

"I don't even want to hear about it." Haley groaned. She wasn't about to touch that line with a ten-foot pole!

"Not even about the time she asked me to play doctor and showed me her—"

"Stop!" Haley cried, covering her ears teasingly. "No more tales from your sordid past. I don't know if I could stand it!" Grasping his arm firmly, she propelled him back to the table that held their typewriters and pushed him down, none too gently, into his chair.

"What's the matter?" asked Adam, his gray eyes glinting wickedly. "Competition a little much for you?"

"Don't flatter yourself," Haley muttered. Reaching around him, she picked up a piece of typing paper from the box on the table and rolled it through his machine, hoping he would take the hint. "So her name was Melissa, was it?" she mused thoughtfully, straightening once more to stand beside him. Gazing downward, she shook her head fondly. "I guess even then, at the tender age of eight, you must have been running true to type."

"Oh?" Adam glanced up curiously. "What type is that?"

"You know what I mean," Haley declared, waving her hand

airily. "The type that goes along with names like that—Melissa, Sheila, Stephanie, Diana. They're all the same. . . ."

Nodding to himself in sudden comprehension, Adam strove to suppress a smile. "Is this going to be another one of your 'tall, blonde and stacked' lectures?"

Haley's telltale blush gave her away, and Adam grinned outright.

"One thing's for sure," he countered. "Certainly no one would ever think of type casting you on account of your name. It's quite unusual, Haley," he said slowly as if turning the name over in his mind. "What sort of woman do you suppose would go along with a name like that?"

"Hard and fast," Haley retorted quickly, then laughed out loud at the expression that crossed Adam's face.

He raised one eyebrow fractionally. "Would you care to explain," he inquired, "or is that a private joke?"

"You know—the comet," she said, still chuckling. "That's what I was named after."

"Halley's comet?" Adam echoed incredulously.

Haley nodded. "My father's always been a bit of an astronomy buff," she explained with a careless shrug. "All I can say in his defense is that it must have seemed like a good idea at the time." Leaning closer, she confided, "Although, believe me, there were times when I was younger when I wasn't nearly so lenient. It's no picnic when you're in grade school and the other kids find out you were named after a piece of flying rock."

"Oh, I don't know," Adam said smoothly, the ghost of a smile beginning to play about his lips. "Actually, I think your father showed remarkable foresight in his choice." Reaching out, he cupped the rounded curve of her buttock and gave a lecherous squeeze. "Somehow he must have known that you were going to have a memorable tail."

Taken by surprise, Haley gasped, then twisted fluidly away. "Dirty old man," she muttered under her breath, just loud enough so that Adam was sure to hear.

But her cheeks glowed with pleasure at his praise, and the

warm, tingling imprint left by the touch of his hand lasted long after she had retaken her seat and turned her thoughts back to work once more.

Go with the flow. That was the phrase that kept popping into Haley's mind with alarming regularity over the course of the next few days, popping unannounced into her thoughts at odd, unexpected moments and teasing her with the seductive quality of its appeal. No doubt about it, the idea was a tempting one.

How nice it would be, Haley thought, just for once to disregard logic, to put aside all notion of what she should or shouldn't do, to simply float and see where life's whims would take her. After all, it wasn't as if she could really get herself into trouble. This was Adam they were talking about—her friend, her confidante, her protector.

Abruptly, that thought brought her up short. Looking at the situation rationally, she had to admit those were all the reasons why she ought to be putting a stop to these fanciful thoughts immediately—now, before they had a chance to get out of hand. And yet Haley knew that she wouldn't, that she didn't want to. For, perversely, they were also all the same reasons that made her feel supremely safe in his care.

They had so much going for them already. It seemed only logical to believe that physical intimacy could only deepen the understanding and affection they felt for one another, add an extra dimension to the closeness they already shared. What could be the harm in that? Then, when the affair had run its course, they would still have their friendship to fall back on—a mature, mellow relationship that had now come full circle.

Still and all, Haley realized, as ideas went, it was far from perfect. It was one thing to know what she wanted, but how about what Adam felt? For all she knew, he might truly have been doing research and simply gotten carried away by the moment. Or worse still, what if he was acting out Rex's needs in the same way she seemed to have assumed Allegra's?

There were simply too many questions, Haley thought with a frown, and no answers in sight for any of them.

Go with the flow, her thoughts repeated seductively. For once, just let nature take its course. Lie back and see what happens rather than trying to choreograph every move, map out every contingency.

I will, thought Haley, filled with sudden resolve. I'll do it! All at once, she felt enormously buoyed by her decision. Just a small, uncomplicated fling; that's all it would be. No more than the natural culmination of the feelings they already shared. She could handle that—no problem! Determinedly, Haley pushed all doubts aside. As to any snags that might arise in their working relationship, well, to repeat one of her father's favorite sayings, she'd just have to burn that bridge when she came to it!

Friday was a beautiful, warm, sunny day—the perfect sort of day for going sailing on the Sound, or so Adam informed her when he arrived in midmorning.

"Think of it!" he exclaimed enthusiastically. "The sun on our faces, the wind at our backs. It'll be great!"

Shaking her head, Haley suppressed a shudder. "Your definition of great and mine must differ radically. A perfect day for sailing," she said thoughtfully. "Are you sure that isn't a contradiction in terms?"

The look Adam gave her was filled with reproach, and immediately Haley felt contrite. He'd been looking forward to this scene eagerly for weeks, she knew. And to be fair, the way he'd envisioned it was wonderful. Against the backdrop of their steamy island paradise, Rex and Allegra were to spend a day sailing, a romantic sojourn on the high seas that would culminate in their making love for the first time.

The only hitch was neither one of them knew the first thing about sailing. Always a stickler for detail, Adam had decided that for authenticity's sake they must learn the basics, acquiring at least enough firsthand knowledge to carry off the background material with aplomb. To this end, a friend had been prevailed upon to supply a boat. A small craft of some sort that Haley had yet to see, although to her mind they were all very much alike, anyway. It was, at this moment, waiting for them on the narrow strip of beach at the bottom of the hill.

"Now, Haley," said Adam with an exaggerated show of patience, "you've got to try and keep an open mind." Taking her hand, he led her out the back door and across the terrace, then started down the hill toward the beach. "How you can live right on the Sound as you do and still not appreciate what it has to offer is beyond me."

"I do appreciate it," Haley shot back quickly. "But it just so happens that I do so visually. Just because I enjoy watching the sun rise over the water doesn't mean I have any desire to risk life and limb by going out there myself."

"Who said anything about risking life and limb?" asked Adam, his voice low and soothing. "Why, I'll bet you won't even get your toes wet."

Oh, yeah? Haley thought suspiciously as she followed him across the lawn. If that was so, then why had he insisted that she wear a bathing suit?

At that thought, a deliciously wicked smile curved her lips upward. Though she'd followed his instructions, judging from the look on Adam's face when she'd greeted him at the door that morning, the end result hadn't been exactly what he'd had in mind. The suit she'd picked stopped just this side of decency—a tiny black crocheted string bikini that hugged the curves of her diminutive figure with loving accuracy. Three small scraps of material held in place by sheer will power and little else. Just let him try and keep his mind on some old boat while she was wearing that!

Then again, Haley mused dreamily, her eyes trained on the rippling play of muscles across Adam's broad shoulders, his attire was hardly the stuff to promote decent thoughts and moral, upright behavior, either. Once upon a time, long ago, she supposed that the skimpy pair of cutoffs he was wearing

might have been a perfectly normal, God-fearing pair of jeans.
But time and much use had taken their toll, and the denim that
remained was shrunken, sun bleached and baby soft. As he
walked, the shorts rode low on his hips, the supple material
hugging the sloping curve of his buttocks intimately.

Yes, indeed, thought Haley, nodding to herself. By all
accounts, this was shaping up to be a very interesting boat ride.

"Voilà!" cried Adam, and Haley pulled her gaze away,
surprised to realize that they had reached the beach already. It
was then that she saw the object of his enthusiasm for the first
time. Immediately, she stopped dead in her tracks, staring in
open-mouthed amazement at the supposedly seaworthy vessel
that was to carry them out onto the Sound.

"What on earth is that?" she demanded, all her instincts for
survival ordaining that she take a hasty step backward. Maybe
there was still time to escape, she thought wildly. Because one
thing was sure—there was no way she was going anywhere on
that precarious-looking thing!

"It's a catamaran," Adam explained easily. Grasping her arm
firmly, he led her forward once more. "A Hobie Cat, to be
exact. Haven't you ever seen one before?"

"No," Haley answered bluntly, her tone clearly conveying
the wish that she wasn't seeing one now.

Frowning, she reached out tentatively to touch one of the
large fiberglass hulls that constituted most of the craft. Between
those and the colorful red and yellow sail that fluttered over-
head, there was nothing else save a small raised platform.
Surely they weren't meant to ride there, were they?

"I only have one question," she announced belligerently.
"Where's the rest of it?"

"The rest of what?" asked Adam, blissfully oblivious to her
dismay. He took the bag holding the few supplies they had
brought with them and secured it to the side of the boat.

"You know," Haley stammered. "The top, the bottom, the
sides, the deck—all those pertinent things."

Adam turned to look at her as though she were only two

steps short of moron. "Top," he said patiently, pointing to the sail. "Bottom." He pointed to the twin hulls. "Deck." He patted the small canvas platform happily. "Otherwise known as the trampoline."

Not at all reassured, Haley peered at the catamaran dubiously. "You mean you actually expect me to sit on *that?*"

"Both of us," Adam confirmed.

"It's got no sides," Haley pointed out, but already she was beginning to feel inevitability settle around her neck like a noose.

"Who needs sides?"

"I do," Haley muttered under her breath, but the objection was pointedly ignored. Louder, she added, "I don't think that thing's big enough to hold both of us. Are you sure we're going to fit?"

"No problem," Adam said blithely. "So we'll be cozy."

"Cozy," Haley said succinctly, "consists of such things as roaring fires and down comforters and snuggling together on dry land." Glaring at him, she gestured at the little boat derisively. "Take my word for it, Adam. There is nothing about this whole thing that even remotely resembles cozy!"

"Tsk tsk tsk." Adam shook his head reprovingly. "Remember what I said about keeping an open mind?" He patted the tramp and reached out to give her a hand. "Come on, up you go."

Desperately, Haley tried one last stall for time. "Are you sure we couldn't put them on a large yacht?" she asked, her voice rising shrilly as she found herself being propelled upward into place. "Or better yet, on a nice land-locked bed?"

"Anyone could write a love scene that way," Adam said dismissively. Digging his heels into the sand, he pushed the boat off the beach and into the water, and Haley grabbed frantically for a hold on the slippery vinyl-covered deck. "But ours is going to be different. Better. Think of it—the fresh salt air, the deep blue water, the fluttering sail and nobody around for miles. It will be wonderfully romantic!"

Abruptly, Haley gulped as Adam hopped up out of the shallow water and pulled himself aboard, and the boat heeled precariously to one side. Then he sat down beside her, and it righted itself once more.

"We could use our imaginations," she suggested faintly.

"Nonsense!" Adam scoffed. His brow furrowed in concentration, he steered the craft out of the congested harbor area. "Haven't you ever heard of hands-on experience?"

If Haley hadn't been so busy praying, she would have laughed out loud. For all Adam's apparent dedication to the craft, she had a sneaking suspicion that wasn't all he was hoping to get his hands on! Not that she had any objections, mind you, but how could she possibly relax and enjoy what was going on when they were perched above a body of deep water on such a treacherously small space? Surely Rex and Allegra could have found some place better than this to get romantic!

"Oh, for Pete's sake!" she said crossly. "Don't you think you're carrying your need for realism a bit far? After all, we didn't have to build anything to write *Love Yourself, Love Your House,* did we?"

"No," Adam conceded. Having piloted the cat out into the open waters of the Sound, he relaxed back against the tramp, looking enormously pleased with himself. "But remember how many carpenters and builders we interviewed? Think of it this way—this time we can be our own experts."

"Really?" Haley purred suggestively. This was a love scene they were rehearsing, after all. "So now you're calling yourself an expert, eh? Don't you think you ought to let me be the judge of that?"

"Behave yourself, woman!" Adam admonished, but a devilish gleam belied the severity of his words. "You'd better show a little respect for the captain; otherwise, you just might find yourself walking the plank!"

Much to her surprise, Haley quickly discovered that the whole experience wasn't nearly as bad as she had imagined it might be. After ten minutes of clinging nervously to the edge of their precarious perch, she developed a cramp in one hand and abandoned that idea in favor of shifting her weight in time to the small craft's rhythm. Five minutes after that, she had the routine down well enough that she was able to sit back comfortably and even begin to enjoy the ride. Soon her initial misgivings were all but forgotten, and she followed Adam's lead eagerly, experimenting with the tiller and the sail until they both had mastered the basic technique of piloting the boat.

After that, it was pure fun all the way. One hour slipped into the next as the catamaran sailed effortlessly about in the calm, clear water. Bearing their inexperience in mind, they were careful not to go too far out, always keeping the shoreline somewhere in sight. Still, the open expanse of deep blue water all around them prompted a feeling of isolation and of privacy. Confident in their abilities, they relaxed, stretching out side by side on the small platform to bask in the sun's hot rays.

"Coming about," Adam announced sometime later. Sitting up, he shifted the sail to change the catamaran's direction.

"What does that mean?" Haley asked languidly, opening one eye as he scooted across the tramp and ducked beneath the boom.

"It means watch out, or you might get hit on the head."

"Oh." Haley nodded, closing her eye once more. Then, suddenly, she frowned. Rolling over, she braced herself up on one elbow and stared at Adam intently.

"You're very pink," she said thoughtfully. "You know, virgin skin like yours probably shouldn't have this kind of exposure." Reaching up, she pressed the top of his shoulder with the tip of her finger and watched the skin turn from red to white, then back to pink. "Does that hurt?"

"A little." Adam shrugged.

Sitting up, Haley reached for the bag of supplies that Adam had secured to the side of the boat. "A little." She snorted inelegantly. "Now is not the time for the strong, silent approach. If we don't do something about that soon, you're going to be burned to a crisp. I hope you've got some sort of lotion in this bag of tricks; otherwise, it's going to be back to terra firma for you."

"Never fear. There's a whole tube of sun block in the bottom of the bag." Adam grinned. "And if you ask me very nicely, I might even let you have the honor of rubbing it on my gorgeous body."

"Oh, yeah?" Haley smirked. She found the plastic bottle and dribbled some cream into the palm of her hand, then slapped it heartily onto his shoulder. "And if you ask *me* very nicely, I just might see to it that you don't suffer too badly in the process."

"Ouch!" cried Adam, pretending to shrink away. "That hurt."

"Things that are good for you are supposed to hurt," Haley said teasingly as she settled down cross-legged behind him. "Didn't your Sunday school teachers ever tell you that?"

"No," Adam grumbled ungraciously. "Where did you go to Sunday school, anyway—Our Lady of the Spartans?"

"Shhh." Haley concentrated on pouring some more of the cool lotion into her palms and working it across his back and shoulders soothingly. "Don't bother the masseuse. Otherwise, she might get mad, and then where would you be?"

"Ummm," said Adam. He was nothing if not a fast learner. Sighing loudly, he leaned back into the gentle motion of her hands. "That feels wonderful."

"Now you're getting the idea," Haley crooned.

A devilish light glittered in the depths of her eyes, and she leaned forward deliberately, her face hovering mere inches behind his shoulder, the cool flow of her breath tickling the back of his neck. Then, succumbing to temptation, she reached out gently—so gently that she wasn't even sure whether he could feel it or not—and ran the tip of her tongue along the back edge of his ear in a delicately provocative caress.

Immediately, Adam stiffened, and just as quickly, Haley pulled away. By the time he had turned around to gaze at her suspiciously, she was once more composed, sitting upright behind him and busying herself with the sun block.

"Something the matter?" she inquired, raising one eyebrow innocently.

The look on Adam's face said everything and nothing as he shook his head.

"Then lie down for me, will you? I want to put some of this on your legs as well."

Silently, Adam obeyed, his body sprawling out along the entire length of the tramp. Haley waited until he was settled, then straddled his hips, facing backward as she began to smooth the cream onto the backs of his thighs. Slowly, she worked her way down the long length of his legs, her hands stroking lightly, her fingers thrilling to the feel of his firm, sun-warmed flesh. Leaning forward, she massaged from thigh to knee, then down over his calves until she reached his ankles and started back once more.

Technically, Haley reflected, the return trip was entirely unnecessary. Already she had applied a lavish coating of the cool, soothing lotion, more than enough to provide the protection Adam needed. Then again, she thought, gazing down at his body stretched out so invitingly beneath her, who was she to deny such opportunity?

Deliberately, her motions slowed, the firm stroke of her hands softening to the feather-light caress of a lover's touch. Using just the tips of her fingers, Haley traced the outline of the muscle that delineated his calf, then skated briefly, teasingly, over the backs of his knees. Then her hands moved upward over his thighs, and she settled back down firmly atop his buttocks once more, her legs doubled under to hug the sides of his hips.

Beneath her, Adam shifted restlessly, and she heard a small, barely perceptible groan. So she was getting to him, was she? thought Haley, smiling to herself. Good. For there was no doubt in her mind that she was getting to herself as well.

All pretense of practicality was now abandoned as Haley let her fingers roam at will, delighting in the feel of the smooth skin beneath her hands and the corded muscles that constricted into hard bands at her touch. With tantalizing slowness, she explored his legs, her hands moving ever upward over his thighs until they reached the fuzzy band of material that marked the bottom cuff of his denim cutoffs.

What a wonderful body Adam had, Haley mused dreamily. Broad shoulders and trim hips. Lean, yet not too thin. And if the kiss they had shared was anything to go by, he knew how to use it as well . . .

There was a sensuous, almost languid quality to the motion as her fingers began to move once more. For several moments, they were content to trace the boundary of his shorts; then, seemingly of their own volition, they strayed beneath it, dipping provocatively under the fabric to tease their way into the depths beyond.

The hiss of Adam's sharply indrawn breath brought Haley out of her reverie with a start. Immediately, her hands stilled, then withdrew. Looking back over her shoulder, she found him gazing up at her as well, his features contorted in something resembling pain. Quickly, then, she slid down from her perch to sit cross-legged beside him, frowning uncertainly. Surely she couldn't have been *that* heavy, could she? Or was his sunburned skin perhaps bothering him more than he'd let on?

"I think that's enough lotion on the back," said Adam, his voice sounding curiously hoarse, and all at once Haley realized what was wrong.

"Oh?" she said innocently, biting back a smile. "Would you like me to put some on the front, then?"

There was a long pause before Adam replied. "I don't think that would be wise just now," he said carefully. "In fact, I think I'd better not turn over at all."

Assimilating that bit of information, Haley grinned. "Oh, dear, have I embarrassed you?" she asked teasingly. "Now, Adam, don't tell me you're shy!"

"No," Adam growled, still lying face downward on the

tramp. "Shy is the last word I'd use to describe what I'm feeling right now. And unless you want to hear graphic details, I suggest you stop asking silly questions."

"Yes, sir, boss," Haley crooned, her tone one of exaggerated obeisance. "No more back talk from me, boss."

"That's better," said Adam, and Haley judged from the slight shift of his shoulders that he was beginning to relax.

Actions speak louder than words, anyway, she thought mischievously, reaching out to trace the line of his shorts once more, this time from the top.

In a flash, Adam rolled over and grasped her wrist. "You, woman, may be the death of me yet!"

"Perhaps," Haley conceded, her eyes glinting humorously. "But you'll have the time of your life dying!"

"I may at that." Adam nodded. Using his weight as a lever, he pulled her down beside him. "You know, now that we know how to sail this thing, there's really only one detail of the scene that we haven't worked out yet."

"Really?" Haley commented, knowing full well what was coming. "And what might that be?"

"Guess," Adam invited softly. He pushed her shoulders down until she lay on her back on the canvas tramp, then levered himself into position above her.

"Does this mean we're coming to the hands-on part of the experience?" Haley asked sweetly.

"Got it in one," Adam murmured.

Haley's eyelids fluttered shut as his lips came down to cover hers, gently at first and then with a growing force that refused to be denied. Her lips parted to his touch, and her tongue welcomed his, joining them in a series of intoxicating kisses. Teasing, tasting, they plundered each other's mouths until Haley could feel the depth of his passion and her own, which spiraled to meet it.

Winding her arms around Adam's neck, she splayed her fingers across his back, seeking out the smooth muscles that rippled between his shoulders. His leg slipped over hers.

pinning her in place, and Haley writhed sensuously beneath him, reveling in the feel of his warm, naked flesh against her own. The harsh mat of hair covering his chest teased her breasts through the thin material of her bikini, and they swelled in response, inviting his attention.

Immediately, the hand that had cradled her chin slid slowly down her throat, then across the smooth, honeyed skin of her chest as Adam used the tip of one finger to trace the upper edge of her crocheted top in a tantalizing caress that mirrored those she had used to torment him earlier.

"That's some bathing suit you're almost wearing," he growled appreciatively. "It's been driving me crazy all afternoon."

Haley opened her mouth to reply but gasped instead, her sudden intake of breath coming as Adam reached nimbly around her back to unfasten the single tie that held the bra in place. In one quick motion, he had swept the top away, and his hand had taken its place. Warmly, he gazed down upon her, his eyes alight with wonder.

"Beautiful," he whispered reverently. "Absolutely perfect."

Then his lips found hers once more, and Haley surrendered herself fully to the potent, heady power of his embrace. Colored lights flashed in the darkness behind her closed eyelids. For the first time in her life, she was dazed by reaction, unable to resist, to move, to think; unable to do anything save glory in the profound impact he was having on her senses.

His hand stroked her breast gently, cupping its weight, while his fingers coaxed the nipple to hardness, brushing back and forth, then tightening around the hard bud until Haley moaned, pressing her head back into the pliant deck and arching her body upward into his hands. Her head began to spin, her mind reeling under the passionate intensity of Adam's lovemaking, and Haley grasped his shoulders, holding them tightly in her hands as if they, and they alone, were the anchor that could hold her steady against the exquisite knot of sensation she felt building inside.

Adam's lips released hers, his breathing ragged and uneven as his head dipped down to nuzzle her throat, then traveled downward still until his mouth settled triumphantly over the prize it sought. Haley gasped, alive with glorious sensation. The sweetly insistent pull of his lips at her breast sent waves of desire coursing through her veins, generating a pulsating heat that radiated throughout her entire body.

"Oh, my God," she murmured. "Adam, please—"

At that moment, the catamaran rocked wildly beneath them, dipping and swaying and tumbling them apart as the tramp on which they lay changed from a flat surface to a sharply angled tilt in only a matter of seconds.

Later, they would realize that their inattention was to blame for what happened—that while their thoughts were elsewhere, the wind had changed direction and the sailboat, following its dictates, had wandered directly into the path of an oncoming wave. But Haley knew only that one moment she and Adam were poised on the brink of a rapture so intense that she could not even begin to imagine its beauty and that the next, the boat was listing precariously to one side, pulling them from one another's arms. Instinctively, their fingers scrambled over the smooth surface, seeking purchase.

"What the hell—!" Frowning ferociously, Adam raised himself up on his hands to see what was wrong. Just then, the sail swung around from high to low, passing harmlessly over Haley's head but catching Adam a glancing blow to the chest. With a startled grunt, he lost his hold and went tumbling over the side of the boat down into the cold blue water below.

Its turn now complete, the catamaran righted itself, and immediately Haley rolled to the edge of the deck to peer down over the side where Adam had disappeared. As she watched, his head broke through to the surface, the once unruly curls plastered flat against his skull, beads of water running down either side of his face and dripping from his eyelashes. Swearing eloquently under his breath, he grabbed hold of the hull, bobbing along in the water beside the craft as he reached up impatiently to rake back the slick strands of hair that had fallen down into his eyes.

Her initial fears allayed, Haley curled her fingers around the edge of the tramp and glowered down at him angrily, fighting down a fierce sense of frustration. She was aching, and her temper rose to assuage that ache. It was all Adam's fault! He was the one who had made her come out on this damn boat in the first place. And now look what had happened!

"The fresh salt air, the deep blue water, the fluttering sail," she said caustically, quoting his own words back at him. "How very romantic!"

Looking up at her, Adam scowled. "What's the matter with you?" he demanded. "I'm the one who's all wet."

There was a certain amount of logic to that point, but Haley refused to let her anger be deflected. "Well, it was a damn inconvenient time for you to take a swim no matter which side you look at it from!" she snapped.

"Tell me about it!" Adam growled, his anger beginning to match her own. Taking a firm hold of the slippery hull, he started to haul himself up out of the water.

A stray breeze washed over the craft, which was listing again under the burden of Adam's weight; and Haley, feeling the cool air on her body, became suddenly aware of her state of undress.

"Oh, damn!" she cried, looking desperately around the small surface of the tramp. The top half of her bikini was nowhere in sight.

"Now what?" Adam was panting heavily, the exertion of pulling himself out of the water making itself felt. On the third try, he managed to slither his legs up onto the hull, then reached up with one hand to seek out a hold on the side of the deck.

"The top of my bathing suit—it's gone! You must have taken it overboard with you when you went."

Balancing precariously between the wet, slippery hull and the deck, Adam grinned devilishly.

As far as Haley was concerned, it was the last straw. "It's not funny!" she cried. Without stopping to think, she reached out and gave his shoulders, which had just cleared the deck, a mighty shove, then watched with satisfaction as Adam toppled back down into the cold water with a sharp cry. "I'll be damned if I'm going to get off this boat in Belle Haven wearing little more than a full-length blush!"

Her anger vented, Haley suddenly felt contrite. Resting on her hands and knees, she peered down over the edge of the deck once more. Almost immediately, Adam surfaced, giving his head a sharp shake, which tossed the hair back out of his eyes and sprayed Haley with a fine mist of cold water.

"Is it safe to come up now?" he asked, looking up at her quizzically.

Frowning ruefully, Haley nodded. She sat back to give him room, her arms crossed self-consciously over her breasts.

"I myself find the possibility of your going topless quite intriguing," Adam announced as he pulled himself up onto the hull once more. This time, Haley forced herself to suffer his mocking grin stoically. But damn it! she thought as his gaze raked over her body. He was really pushing his luck!

"However, as I was about to point out before I was so rudely interrupted—" He paused for effect, frowning sternly in Haley's direction. "The blush will be entirely unnecessary, as I have the missing item right here."

Having finally reached the safety of the deck, Adam held one hand aloft triumphantly, and Haley saw that he'd had her top the entire time. The tiny wisps of material dangled from his fingers, wafting in the slight breeze. "The strings must have been tangled around my fingers," he explained with a shrug, sounding not the least bit contrite.

"Well, why didn't you say so?" Haley snapped. Rising up on her knees, she snatched the top from his upraised hand, an act that dictated not only that she uncover herself but also that she lean into his body, her naked breasts quivering mere inches away from his face.

"Nice view," Adam commented pleasantly.

It was then that Haley began to laugh, the pent-up frustrations of the last few moments finally venting themselves in a flurry of giggles that racked her slender body and reduced her intake of breath to great gasping gulps. The crocheted top lay momentarily forgotten in hands that had gone limp. Sitting cross-legged before him, Haley laughed until tears of merriment rolled down her face.

At first, Adam could only stare at her in utter amazement, his expression clearly conveying his belief that if she wasn't out of her mind, she was certainly close. Then, finally, he joined in as well, shaking his head in rueful acknowledgment of the ludicrous situation they had gotten themselves into. Moving over beside her, he picked up the bra and slipped it into place, reaching gently around to knot the strings together behind her back.

"Some fine sailors we turned out to be," Haley said, gasping for breath.

"Now, now, we weren't doing all that badly," Adam disagreed with a mock show of sternness. "In fact, as I recall, we were doing quite well until someone who shall remain nameless decided to practice her feminine wiles on my poor, unsuspecting body."

"Surely you don't mean me!" Haley sputtered, pretending to be outraged. "Are you trying to say that *I* was the one responsible for starting that?"

Adam nodded twice for emphasis.

"Is that so?" she demanded, eyebrows arched skeptically. "Then how come you were the one who was on top? In fact, as *I* remember it, you were holding me in place."

"A mere technicality." Adam shrugged. "You have to admit it was the only gentlemanly thing to do. After all, I was the one wearing all the sunscreen. And thanks to you, only one side of me was covered. So you see, I really didn't have any choice in the matter at all."

"Hmph," Haley snorted expressively. "That is without a

doubt one of the flimsiest excuses I've ever heard. Besides, who was it who shanghaied me out onto the bounding main in the first place? You know full well that if it had been up to me, we would never have left dry land at all." Steadily, the magnitude of Haley's complaint grew, gathering momentum as it went along. "I told you this was impractical. I told you it wouldn't work—"

"Okay, I admit it—you were right," Adam conceded, but his gray eyes still glittered with amusement. "Next time, I guess I'll just have to believe you, without going in for any graphic demonstrations."

"Good." Haley nodded, pointedly ignoring any hints that he might not be totally serious. Reaching around behind her, she grasped the tiller and turned the catamaran toward shore.

"Poor Rex," Adam muttered under his breath, his tone laced with such concern that Haley glanced back over her shoulder.

"What on earth are you mumbling about?"

"Our poor, beleaguered hero," said Adam, shaking his head mournfully. "It seems he's not going to get quite what he hoped for out of his sailing trip, either. After all, since we have firsthand experience of the difficulties involved, I don't think it would be fair of us to leave the scene the way we originally envisioned it."

"I see what you mean," Haley said, chewing her lip thoughtfully.

"As near as I can tell, that poor man must be feeling frustrated as all hell right about now."

Looking at him, Haley's eyes narrowed speculatively. "Now who's taking their character's role to heart?" she wondered aloud.

But Adam, recognizing the rhetorical question for what it was, declined to answer, and Haley was left to ponder that uneasy thought all the way back to shore.

6

Over the weekend, Haley didn't see Adam at all.

A great-aunt who lived in Pennsylvania was having her hundredth birthday, and Morgans from all up and down the East Coast were gathering in Harrisburg to celebrate with a lavish two day family get-together. It was late Sunday evening before she managed to get away and, after five hours on the road, early Monday morning before she reached home and fell into bed, thoroughly exhausted.

By the time she awoke, bright sunlight was streaming in through her open bedroom window, the clock on the night stand confirmed that it was after noon, and the steady clickety-click of a typewriter in the next room attested to the fact that Adam had used his own key to let himself in and gone to work without her.

The odor of freshly brewed coffee filled the air, and Haley sniffed the aroma appreciatively. Tossing off the light sheet that covered her, she hopped out of bed and padded across the room naked. Just inside the closet door hung an embroidered raw silk kimono that served as a bathrobe. She pulled it on, tying the sash securely about her waist, then combed through her hair with her fingers and sauntered out into the next room.

"Well, it's about time," Adam greeted her. He glanced up casually as her door opened, his fingers continuing to fly over the keys. "I know the term free-lance implies that you can set your own schedule, but don't you think you might be carrying things just a bit far?"

"Late night last night." Haley shrugged, leaning down to peer at the sheaf of word-covered pages that lay stacked next to his typewriter. "I didn't get in until almost four."

Adam arched one eyebrow speculatively but declined to comment as he continued typing.

"Besides," Haley added, thumbing through the pages, "from the looks of all this, you're doing quite all right by yourself."

"Necessity," Adam quoted solemnly, "is the mother of invention. But that doesn't mean that I'm willing to hold up your end indefinitely. In fact, I'd say your lady-of-leisure act is just about over. Already I feel my benevolence starting to fade. You've got ten minutes, no more, and if I were you, I'd put that time to good use." Teasingly, he reached out to tweak the sash of her robe, the only thing standing between her and full revelation. "Because if you want us to get any work done at all, you'll damn well start by getting dressed."

"Yes, boss," Haley said meekly. But a flippant grin belied her words as she slapped his hand away and whirled on her heel, marching back to her bedroom for a quick shower and a change of clothing.

Ten minutes later, she was back, now suitably attired in a red linen camp shirt and a pair of white designer jeans. Walking past him into the kitchen, she rummaged through the refrigerator in search of something to eat.

"Time's up," Adam announced sternly from the next room. "Get your butt in here, kid."

"In a minute," Haley mumbled, the words garbled by the corn muffin she held between her lips. Quickly, she pulled out the butter and a bottle of orange juice to complete the meal.

"Haley!" Adam's accusing voice drifted in as she buttered the muffin and poured the juice. "How do you expect me to work when you're in there loafing?"

"I don't," she called back, stuffing the muffin into her mouth.

She thumbed quickly through the morning paper, searching for the crossword puzzle. "You know me. I'm a great believer in equal-opportunity loafing. Why don't you come in and join me?"

"I've got a better idea," said Adam, appearing in the doorway. "Why don't *you* come in and join me?"

"Slave driver," Haley muttered under her breath, barely managing to snatch up the puzzle and her glass of juice as he grasped her other hand and dragged her into the dining room. "You really ought to try and curb these cave-man tendencies of yours," she grumbled resignedly. Adam pushed her down into her chair, then walked around the table to take his own seat at the other end. "I can't imagine they make a very good impression on your dates."

"Oh, I don't know." Adam smiled across at her. "Yours is the first complaint I've had." He took in a deep breath, and his chest swelled to massive proportions as he raised one arm and flexed his muscles for her benefit. "Some women like the forceful type."

Laughing delightedly, Haley shook her head. "Has anyone ever told you you're hopeless?"

"My mother," Adam allowed, "has been known to share that opinion on occasion."

"Perceptive woman, your mother," Haley mused aloud.

"Then again," Adam said earnestly, "she also tells me I'm damn cute."

"A thoroughly unbiased opinion, I'm sure."

"Thoroughly," Adam agreed solemnly.

"Well, then," Haley said slowly. She leaned closer as if confiding a great secret. "If you promise not to tell anybody, I'll tell you something about your mother."

Obligingly, Adam bent closer as well to listen.

Cupping her hand around her mouth, Haley whispered in his ear, "She's right!"

Laughing together, they settled back into their respective chairs, Adam immediately resuming his typing, while Haley picked up her pen and began to frown thoughtfully over the crossword puzzle nestled on her lap. Ten minutes passed quickly, and then another five. Each was totally absorbed in what they were doing.

Glancing up, Haley smoothed back a lock of hair and tucked it behind her ear absently. "What do you suppose is a five-letter word for onager?" she mused.

"I don't know." Adam frowned as he met her gaze. "What does onager mean?"

Haley shrugged expressively. "I'm not exactly sure. I think it's some kind of a donkey."

"A donkey?" Adam repeated, his tone doubtful. "What donkey? What are you talking about? I don't recall having any donkeys in this scene." His lips tightening into a straight line, he gazed at her sternly. "Are you going off on one of your tangents again? I thought we agreed Rex and Allegra were on their way to a disco."

"Relax." Haley grinned. "I didn't put any donkeys in your disco scene. Onager is the clue for number thirty-four down."

"Down what?" asked Adam, his bewilderment obvious.

"Down the crossword puzzle," Haley said slowly, as if explaining something perfectly obvious. Reaching down, she held up the paper that had been sitting on her lap. "See?"

"Are you serious? Do you mean to tell me that all this time I've been working, typing my poor fingers to the bone, you've been sitting there doing a *crossword puzzle?*" Thoroughly incredulous, he spoke the last two words as though they were some sort of hideous affliction.

"Actually," Haley said mildly, "most of the time you've been working, I was asleep. Then trying unsuccessfully to eat breakfast. It's only been the last fifteen minutes or so that I've been working on the puzzle." Laying down her pen, she scowled at him accusingly. "And if you don't stop nagging me, I may never get it done!"

"Nagging you?" Adam yelped, his forehead furrowing ominously. *"Nagging you?"*

"I really don't see what you're getting all excited about. You know I need a good crossword puzzle to get me started thinking in the morning. Some people need coffee—" Haley gestured meaningfully at the empty mug that sat beside his typewriter. "I need this. Sometimes I think when I sleep at night, all the words get jumbled up in my brain. There's nothing like a good crossword puzzle to put them back in working order."

Across the table, Adam sighed resignedly. "Why don't you try jenny?" he suggested, and Haley's face brightened.

"Jenny," she repeated, writing it in. "Perfect."

"Good," said Adam. "Now are you done?"

"Not quite." She scribbled furiously, filling in the words that the new addition had given her.

"Yes, you are," Adam said firmly, starting to rise. "Take my word for it."

"Okay, okay, cool your jets," said Haley, tossing the paper aside.

Reaching over, she picked up the stack of pages Adam had typed and skimmed through them quickly. "Now let me see; they're on their way to the night club, right? Let's try a romantic moon-lit walk on the beach. You never know what might lead to bigger and better things . . ."

Eight hours later, they were still working.

A phone call to a local Chinese restaurant had produced an order of takeout food to serve as dinner; and now, with the empty cardboard cartons cleared away and the dishes cleaned and dried, they were once more seated at opposite ends of the table.

"Okay, this is it," Adam announced importantly. "We're three-quarters of the way through the story. I think the time has definitely come for Rex to make his big move."

Resting her elbows on the table, Haley cupped her chin in her hands. "What do you mean by 'big move'?"

"You know—the grand seduction. The love scene par excellence. The pass to end all passes."

"I hate to break it to you," Haley said with a smile, "but this hero of ours has been making passes for the last hundred and fifty pages, and as far as I can tell, he's not any closer to seducing Allegra than he was on page one. For a supposedly liberated lady, she seems to be doing an awfully good job of playing hard to get."

"I know," Adam agreed, his expression mournful. "Clearly, our man is in need of a little outside help. That's why we're about to tip the scales in his favor."

"Oh?" Haley arched one eyebrow curiously. "And just how do you propose we do that?"

"We're going to employ the time-honored tradition of desperate men everywhere," Adam said smugly. Then, seeing that Haley still hadn't the faintest idea what he was talking about, he added, "To put it quite simply, Rex is about to get Allegra drunk."

"Oh, he is, is he?"

Adam grinned boyishly. "You know what they say—candy's dandy, but liquor's quicker."

"Are you drawing from personal experience here?"

Adam leered at her playfully. "Let's just say I have great personal belief in the power of alcohol to lower inhibitions. Otherwise, I'm quite sure I never would have mooned that police car . . ."

"What police car?" asked Haley, perking up interestedly.

Adam waved his hand dismissively. "It's an old story. But back to the matter at hand. I'd have to say that after one hundred and fifty pages of advance and retreat, if there's anyone whose inhibitions sorely need lowering, it's our lady Allegra."

"I don't know," said Haley, stroking her chin thoughtfully. She'd always known Adam was the impulsive sort, but *a police car*? That must have been something to see. Even at her wildest, she'd never have considered doing anything like that! Abruptly, Haley frowned. Maybe that was the problem they'd been having so far. . . .

"What?" asked Adam, watching her closely. "I can see you're building up to something over there."

Haley shook her head uncertainly. "It just doesn't seem fair to me. Do you realize that so far Rex is the one who's gotten to do all the fun things? All the heroics and bits of derring-do have been his."

"As well they should be." Adam shrugged, blithely dismissing her protest.

Across the table, Haley scowled. Clearly, it was time to practice a little assertiveness here, she thought. In fact, it was past time. He sounded so sure of himself. Smug, even complacent. When had things begun to get so out of hand?

"I'll tell you what," she proposed. "If you want to do a scene like that, it's fine with me. But let's approach it from the other way around. At the end of the evening, Allegra is still on her feet, and it's Rex who's drunk himself under the table."

"You've got to be kidding me!" The incredulous expression on Adam's face clearly indicated that he thought her sanity might be in question. "Nobody would believe that! It isn't realistic—there's just no way a woman could outdrink a man! It has to do with mass and body weight—"

"And outdated macho concepts about what's manly and what's not!" Haley shot back, feeling suddenly quite belligerent. Now that she stopped and thought about it, she'd been doing an awful lot of compromising lately. Well, let Adam try giving in for a change, because this was one issue where she wasn't going to back down!

"Machismo has nothing to do with it," Adam said evenly. "It's a well-known fact that men are able to hold their liquor better than women."

"Is that so?" Haley's delicately arched brow indicated her disdain. "Well, then, mister, if you're so sure of your facts, how about putting your money where your mouth is?"

"Gladly!" Reaching down into the pocket of his jeans, Adam pulled out a ten-dollar bill and tossed it on the table.

"Done!" cried Haley, leaping up to match the bill with one

from her purse. Hands on her hips, she glared at him across the table, the money lying like a challenge between them. The scene, the characters, the writing—all were forgotten. In the heat of the moment, nothing mattered save the need to prove Adam wrong.

"My bar is pretty well stocked," she said, crossing the room in three quick strides and pulling open the cabinet in the buffet that housed the liquor. Leaning down, she scanned the bottles. "Name your poison."

Coming up behind her, Adam surveyed the selection for a moment over her shoulder. Then he reached in and picked up a bottle of Jack Daniels and cocked his head questioningly.

"Fine with me." Haley nodded. She shut the door, then opened another and pulled out two tumblers.

Strolling into the living room, she set the glasses down on the coffee table, then sat down on the couch, watching as Adam twisted off the bottle's cap and poured them each a shot.

"I suppose we ought to set some ground rules," said Adam, running his finger around the rim of his glass thoughtfully.

"Ground rules?" Haley echoed in surprise. "For drinking?"

Solemnly, Adam nodded. "Otherwise, we'll never be able to keep things straight. For example, when I do this"—lifting the glass, he swallowed its entire contents in one quick gulp—"then you have to do likewise."

Shaking her head reprovingly, Haley sighed. "You, sir, have no respect for fine sippin' whisky."

"Stalling?" Adam inquired pleasantly.

"Of course not!"

Adam grinned, picking up her glass and handing it to her. "Bottoms up, kid."

Quickly, she tilted back her head and polished off the whisky. The dark amber liquid burned going down, immediately making the first of its effects known.

No matter, Haley thought confidently. She could handle it. This wasn't the first time she'd tossed off a shot of whisky. No, she knew what she was doing, all right. That her body had an inordinately high tolerance to alcohol was one of life's little bonuses that Adam need never know anything about. She may have eaten crow over their last wager, but this time she had him for sure!

Smiling, Haley set the tumbler back down on the table with a loud thump. "Are there any more rules I should know about before we go any further?" she inquired sweetly.

"None that I can think of." Adam refilled both tumblers. "Only that we both have to reach the bottom of our respective glasses at the same time. So if one of us finishes before the other, then whoever's behind has to drink theirs down as well."

"I don't foresee any problem with that," said Haley. Picking up her glass, she tossed down the second shot, then licked her lips dry with an exceedingly feminine display of manners. "Do you?"

"None," Adam agreed with a grin as he lifted his glass to follow suit.

One hour and six shots later, both Adam and Haley were feeling somewhat the worse for wear. The speed of their intake had declined sharply, as had the steadiness of the hands that refilled the glasses. Still and all, Haley knew she was doing pretty well. So what if her brain was a bit foggy, her reactions a little slower than they might have been? From the looks of Adam, who lay sprawled haphazardly on the cream-colored rug, he wasn't faring any better.

"Fill 'er up, barkeep," she ordered. A sudden unexpected giggle erupted, taking her by surprise, and she quickly covered it with a discreet cough. Leaning back languidly against the foot of the couch behind her, Haley pushed the tumbler across the table with the tips of her fingers. When had they gotten down onto the floor, anyway? she wondered muzzily.

"With pleasure," said Adam, rousing himself to splash more whisky into the two glasses. "How are you feeling over there?"

"Wonderful," Haley replied quickly. Picking up a deck of cards from the shelf beneath the coffee table, she began to sort through them idly. "Fit as a fiddle, sharp as a tack and rarin' to go."

"No ill effects yet?"

"None that I can feel." Haley shrugged vaguely, determined to keep up a good front. Glancing over at Adam, she found him propped against the edge of the table, watching her through narrowed eyes.

Surely no one could drink that much liquor that quickly and *not* be feeling the effects, she told herself fiercely. So why did Adam look so good all of a sudden? Was it her imagination, or did he actually seem more alert now than he had for quite some time? It just wasn't possible, she thought with a hasty gulp. Could he be conning her?

"I'm glad to hear you're doing so well," Adam said dryly, and Haley realized she hadn't fooled him for a moment. "In that case, I'd say we're going to be here for quite a while yet. How about a game of cards to pass the time?"

"I don't know," Haley said slowly. She peered at him suspiciously. What was he up to now?

"What's the matter?" Adam taunted her. Supremely nonchalant, he picked up his glass and sipped at the contents, savoring the whisky with obvious relish. "Afraid you couldn't handle it in your present state?"

"What state is that?" asked Haley, denying her inebriation with utmost dignity.

Screwing up his face, Adam thought for a moment before answering. Then, abruptly, his features brightened. "Connecticut," he announced with all due seriousness, and Haley began to giggle. So she wasn't the only one trying to put up a good front!

"Of course I can handle it," Haley declared airily, with a show of false bravado that felt quite convincing. "I can take you on anytime I like."

"Them's fightin' words, woman," Adam growled. He pushed

the table to one side, then sat down cross-legged before her. "Go on, then; deal out the cards."

"In a moment," said Haley, applying herself diligently to shuffling the deck. Good Lord! she thought as several cards flipped out of her hands and flew across the room. So much for manual dexterity! Suddenly, she felt as though her hands had grown ten thumbs.

Adam said nothing, which for the sake of his own survival was fortunate, but his gray eyes glittered with amusement as he retrieved the errant cards and added them back to the deck.

"Thanks, boss," Haley muttered, once again calling on her innate sense of dignity to carry her through. She transferred the deck into one hand, ready to deal, and abruptly realized that she hadn't any idea how many cards to hand out. "What are we playing?" she asked, looking up in confusion.

For a moment, Adam considered the question, and Haley, waiting for his answer, thought fancifully that she could almost see the wheels turning in his head. "What do you know?" he asked finally.

Two can play at this game, Haley decided, taking her time as well. "I play a mean game of gin rummy," she said slowly. "And, of course, there's always old maid."

At that, Adam smiled. "Why is it I get the distinct impression that I'm about to be hustled?"

"Search me," Haley shrugged, the picture of affronted innocence.

The smile had now widened to a full-fledged grin. "Okay, I'll bite. How about poker?"

"If you insist," Haley agreed, her tone deliberately casual. Looking down to hide a satisfied smile that refused to be contained, she began to deal out the cards.

"What's the game?"

"Five card draw," Haley announced calmly, setting the remainder of the deck aside. "Jacks or better to open."

"And to think, she looks like such a sweet young thing," Adam muttered under his breath to no one in particular.

Haley reached down to pick up her cards, but Adam's hand snaked out to stop her. "What are the stakes?" he asked.

"Stakes?" Haley echoed hollowly, wishing fervently that her brain wasn't working in slow motion.

"You know," said Adam. "What are we playing for?"

"Control of the Western world?" Haley jibed, giggling delightedly at her own joke.

"I think not," said Adam, looking suddenly quite a bit more coherent than Haley might have wished for under the circumstances. "Do you have any poker chips?"

"Not a one," she announced, not perturbed in the least by the shortcoming.

"Matches?"

"I don't smoke," said Haley, and for some reason, she found that to be incredibly funny as well.

"Well, then," said Adam with the air of one who has resigned himself to his fate, "I guess it will just have to be our clothes."

"Our clothes?" cried Haley, beginning to giggle anew. "Do you mean to say that you want to play *strip poker?*"

"Why not?" Adam shrugged.

Why not indeed, thought Haley. The idea certainly had intriguing possibilities. Then again, on the other hand, think what a chump she'd feel like if Adam ended up still dressed from head to toe while she took off one piece of clothing after another! Frowning, she chewed her lower lip thoughtfully. No, that possibility wasn't likely. After all, she was a pretty fair poker player. And lucky at cards, as well.

Quickly, unobtrusively, Haley's eyes scanned his body, assessing how many pieces they might each have to lose. If she counted all her jewelry . . .

"Come on," Adam prompted, reaching for his cards. "Where's all that confidence you had a minute ago? Remember," he added persuasively, "only the loser has to undress."

He was sounding insufferably smug again, Haley realized. And she for one couldn't think of anything that would bring him down a peg faster than finding himself stripped down to the buff in the middle of her living-room rug!

"You're on!" she declared, her voice strong with determination. Quickly, she reached for her own hand, as well.

Too bad she couldn't have had a look at what was under there before she made any rash promises, Haley thought a moment later as she studied the truly lackluster collection of cards in her hand.

"I'll take two," said Adam, and she obligingly dealt them out.

Two? Haley thought in dismay, setting aside her ace and drawing four cards for herself. Did that mean he already had three of a kind? Scowling, she considered what to take off first. With a sinking feeling in the pit of her stomach, she lifted her four new cards and spread them slowly in her hand. A six, a nine and then wonder of wonders, two more aces.

For his first forfeit, Adam removed a shoe. The second hand cost him the other shoe. For the third, he unwound his belt. Then, just when from Haley's point of view, things were starting to get interesting, her luck began to change. Holding nothing better than a pair of threes, she lost for the first time.

Slowly and deliberately, she pulled the ring off her little finger and laid it down atop the table.

"What the hell is that supposed to be?" Adam demanded, looking down at the object suspiciously.

"A ring," said Haley, deliberately misunderstanding his meaning. Smiling, she picked up the jewel and held it up to the light. "See? A pretty little opal. My grandmother gave it to me for—"

"I can see it's a ring," Adam interrupted her testily. "What I want to know is, what's it doing on the forfeit pile?"

Haley smiled sweetly as she leaned closer and peered into Adam's eyes. "If you can't figure that one out, then you must be drunker than you think."

Adam muttered something inaudible under his breath that didn't sound promising. Blithely, Haley decided to ignore it.

"I had to take something off," she said. "And I did. This is it."

"Oh, no, you don't," Adam growled. "Jewelry doesn't count."

Stroking her chin with her fingers reflectively, Haley pretended to think. "I don't recall hearing any rules to that effect," she said pleasantly. "I may have had quite a bit to drink, but I'm sure I would have remembered something like that."

Looking back and forth between her and the tiny ring she had placed beside his clothes, Adam glowered belligerently. "Good grief," he groaned, his gaze now roaming from her watch to her earrings to the thin gold chain that circled her neck. "We're going to be here all night."

"Not necessarily," Haley countered sweetly. Taking her time, she looked him up and down as well. A cotton shirt, a pair of jeans, and the underwear beneath them. By her count, he had only three more pieces to go. "You said it yourself, remember? Only the loser has to undress."

With a muffled oath, Adam picked up his tumbler and drained it. "Just my luck, I'm playing strip poker with a woman who's dressed like the Spanish Armada!"

But if Haley thought she had the situation well in hand, she soon learned differently. The luck that had sustained her through the first few hands seemed suddenly to have vanished; and the shot that she drank to match the one Adam tossed down did little to help the coherency of a brain that was already having a hard time distinguishing hearts from diamonds and spades from clubs. In vain, she tried to remember the odds for making each of the various combinations. Then, when that failed, she turned to intuition with equal lack of success.

Over the course of the next six hands, she lost the remainder of her jewelry and her shoes as well. She had used up all her advantage. The stakes were now perfectly even.

On the next deal, Adam drew to an inside straight and lost his shirt, literally.

With a smug grin plastered across her face, Haley watched as he slowly unbuttoned the pink oxford cloth, then shifted to pull

the material free of his waistband. The muscles rippled smoothly across his chest as he tossed the shirt onto the back of the
couch, and suddenly, unaccountably, she felt like a voyeur, a
Peeping Tom stealing a forbidden glimpse of untold pleasures.

Don't be ridiculous! Haley chided herself. She'd certainly
seen Adam bare chested before. Many times, in fact. Yet,
undeniably, there was something about the cozy intimacy of the
situation that made his partial nudity all the more provocative—
the two of them seated only inches apart on the soft rug,
sharing a bottle of liquor that had dulled their senses but at the
same time heightened their awareness. Added to the heady
sense of anticipation engendered by the game itself, it was a
potent combination. A quiver began to ripple through her,
followed by a deliciously erotic sensation of warmth.

Stop it! she warned herself fiercely, but still she was unable to
pull her eyes away. Instead, they lingered quite deliberately on
the man before her, tracing the slope of his broad shoulders, the
sinewed muscles of his chest, the lean, flat stomach, and the
mat of dark brown hair that spiraled downward provocatively
into the waistband of his jeans.

"Just window-shopping?" Adam inquired pleasantly. "Or
were you hoping to buy?"

"What?" Haley glanced up quickly, blinking several times as
if wakening from a wonderful dream. "Did you say something?"

"Not me." Adam grinned. He reached out to pick up the
cards. "Perhaps you'd like to play another hand now?"

As soon as Haley looked at her hand, she knew she was in
trouble. Four different suits, five different denominations, without even the possibility of a straight to give her hope. Even
drawing the maximum three cards allowed, she still came up
with nothing. As the nature of the game precluded bluffing, she
was stuck. Her own shirt was next to go.

It wasn't as if she were actually *naked* or anything, Haley told
herself reassuringly as she unbuttoned the camp shirt and set it
aside.

Early in life she'd discovered that one of the advantages of having a figure so small was that she could wear anything. Other women needed support, shaping—she needed only adornment. Making the most of that bonus, Haley chose her underwear to indulge her fantasies, buying the laciest, most feminine undergarments possible—silk camisoles, satin teddies, and frilly bras whose function was more decorative than practical.

That night, beneath her clothing, she was wearing a teddy, a small, sky-blue garment fashioned out of ribbons and lace that covered everything that needed covering, if only just barely. Proudly, she lifted her head to meet Adam's gaze and found that he was giving her the same sort of thorough perusal she had just given him. If the wolfish gleam in his eye was anything to go by, he wasn't disappointed.

Suddenly, Haley felt a shock of pure desire, of deep, fundamental longing, sweep through her veins. Soon . . . she thought dazedly, reaching for her cards. The game was almost over, and then . . .

On the next deal, she managed a full house, the best hand she'd seen all night, only to be beaten by Adam with four twos.

"Your turn," Adam pointed out unnecessarily. He leaned back on the carpet, his arms crossed behind his head, as if he were preparing himself to enjoy the show.

Fortified by the ample quantities of whisky, Haley refused to let herself be intimidated by his behavior. Gracefully, she stood up and shed her jeans, creasing them carefully before laying them over the back of the couch.

So what? she told herself defiantly. He wasn't seeing anything he hadn't already seen on the beach. So why did she suddenly feel so naked, so vulnerable, before him? As if the game they were playing suddenly had nothing to do with cards and stakes and winning and losing and everything to do with a man and a woman and the elemental forces that had been sparked between them?

"Deal the cards, boss," said Haley, her voice no more than a throaty whisper.

If she couldn't control this devastating awareness, this reckless, fiery need that ran rampant through her veins, then the least she could do was try and put them on an equal footing, Haley decided. She had to win this next hand; she just had to.

But she didn't.

Methodically, Adam gathered up the deck, his eyes lowered, intent on the task. She had lost, but there would be no teasing, no taunting now. He would give her all the time she needed, for he knew she would pay the forfeit. After all, there was honor at stake here.

Stiffly, Haley rose to her feet. Standing above him, she unfastened the first of the buttons between her breasts. Then, suddenly shy, she turned her back before going on. When the teddy hung open, exposing the creamy valley between her high, firm breasts, the rosy-tipped aureolas, which puckered and stiffened, she slipped the satin ribbons from her shoulders and lowered the garment over her hips.

Not a sound came from behind her as the soft, shiny material drifted down her legs and settled into a small blue pool at her feet. Taking a deep breath, Haley drew back her shoulders proudly and decided she was ready. Slowly, majestically, she turned around.

There, sprawled out across the rug, lay Adam. He had passed out cold.

7

When Haley awoke the next morning, she immediately noticed two things. The first was the absence of a hangover, which, by all rights, should have been a beauty. The second— there was a man in her bed. Adam, to be exact. Curled up on his side, his arm draped casually across her breasts, his breathing deep and steady, he was blissfully asleep, still as dead to the world as he had been the night before when she'd dragged him in from the living room, undressed him and placed him under the covers.

"Poor Adam," Haley murmured softly, gazing down on him as he slept. Slowly, tentatively, she reached out with one hand to stroke the clean, sculpted line of his shoulder, marveling that even in repose his body could convey such a sense of strength. "What in the world am I ever going to do with you?" she wondered softly.

The desire to reach out and gather him to her, to cradle him against her breast protectively, was so strong that for a moment Haley almost succumbed to the impulse. Then, fighting down the urge, she settled instead for smoothing back the locks of silky brown hair that had fallen down over his forehead while he slept.

It was then, as she lay beside him, stroking his head tenderly with her hand, that Haley knew the truth. Whether wisdom or folly, whether right or wrong, she had fallen in love with Adam Burke.

So this was how it happened, she mused dreamily. No flashing lights, no ringing bells, no grand revelation. Just an all-encompassing sense of wonder and of joy, a sure and steady knowledge that she would gladly do anything for the man who lay by her side.

Actually, Haley decided, unsure whether to be pleased or not, it was rather like being dropped from a plane without the benefit of a parachute. Exciting, yet terrifying all at once. And who knew where she might land? In fact, only one thing was sure. After this, her life would never be the same.

Up until now, it had all been little more than a game. She had tested the limits of their relationship curiously, playfully, secure in the knowledge that when the game was over, she could retreat back to the safety of their friendship, and nothing would be lost—no feelings hurt, no emotions sacrificed. Yet, suddenly, all that had changed, for Haley knew with certainty that no matter what was to come in the days ahead, no matter where the course of their lives might take them, a part of her would always belong to Adam. Adam, her friend, her partner, her love.

He stirred beside her, and she jumped. Like a startled doe, Haley drew back quickly, watching, waiting. But Adam only moaned and turned over without waking, still blissfully oblivious to her presence.

Emboldened by the new and wondrous feelings washing over her, Haley grinned idiotically, suddenly filled with delight at the thought of giving Adam pleasure. Lying on her side, she braced one elbow on the bed and cradled her head in her palm. Her other hand reached out to caress his chest, tracing a series of ever-widening circles on the warm, hair-roughened flesh.

"Adam," she whispered softly, willing him to hear her and respond. "Are you awake?"

A noise rumbled deep within his throat as Adam shifted once

more. His eyes, however, remained firmly shut. Undeterred, Haley doubled her efforts. The fingers, which roamed over his body in languid exploration, found the flat bud of one male nipple and coaxed it to hardness. Then, following her fingers with her lips, she bent down to stroke him with her tongue, pulling the nipple into her mouth and sucking on it gently.

Again, the noise sounded, a deep, resonant rumbling that seemed drawn from the depths of his chest. Once more Haley drew back, her brow this time furrowed in consternation. What was going on here, anyway? If she didn't know better, she'd think that sounded more like a groan of pain than the moan of pleasure she'd been expecting.

"Adam?" she murmured quizzically, leaning over his body to stare down into his face. "Boss, are you there?"

At that moment, Adam awoke. He opened one eye slowly, agonizingly, and even that small movement seemed to cost him much effort, for no sooner had he seen her hovering above him, than he immediately snapped it shut again. His groan this time was loud and unmistakable.

Terrific, thought Haley, frowning down at him. Somehow that was just not the passionate response she'd been hoping for.

"Where am I?" Adam mumbled, his voice thick.

"You're in my bed." Snuggling closer, Haley pressed her breasts against him meaningfully.

Adam, however, seemed oblivious to the message she was trying to send. "How did I get here?"

Never one to give up easily, Haley leaned down and draped herself across his chest, conscious that the strap to her nightgown had slipped down provocatively off one shoulder. "You lost the bet," she whispered huskily into his ear.

At that unfortunate reminder of the previous night's proceedings, Adam winced. Reaching up, he rubbed his eyes wearily with the back of his hand and then, as if to make his displeasure with the situation clear, groaned loudly once more.

"Are you all right?" asked Haley, her tone suddenly fraught with concern. Was he hung over? she wondered. Was that what was wrong? In her whole life, she'd never fallen victim to that particular curse, so she had no practical experience to draw from, yet what else could be the matter? She was certainly making her intentions clear enough, but Adam wasn't responding at all. By all expectations—and she'd had plenty—he was acting *very* strangely.

"I'm fine," he muttered gruffly. "I just need some time alone, that's all."

Rolling away, Adam slipped off the bed, leaving Haley caught up in the discarded covers. He staggered to the bathroom and latched the door shut behind him without once looking back.

So much for romance, thought Haley, flopping back down onto the pillow disgustedly. She'd always thought that old line about having a headache was supposed to be a joke! Kicking off the covers irritably, she glowered at the closed door. Still, he'd claimed to be fine, so maybe that wasn't the problem at all. . . .

From inside the bathroom came the sound of the shower being turned on full blast. Now what? she wondered. Was she supposed to wait for him? And if so, for how long? And what if he didn't feel any better when he came out than he had when he'd gone in?

If that was the case, thought Haley, she'd simply look like a fool. In fact, if the truth be known, she'd probably crossed that line already. Good God, she couldn't have been any more blatant about what she wanted if she'd served herself up on a silver platter with an apple in her mouth! And look what it had gotten her—she was still sitting around trussed up like a stuffed pig for a man who, to all appearances, wasn't the slightest bit interested!

"If this isn't the damndest situation I've ever been in!" she grumbled out loud to no one in particular. For some reason, it had never even crossed her mind that he might turn her down. But he had, and bluntly, too, without even trying to soften the rejection with tender words or soothing platitudes. No, he'd simply cut and run, as if he couldn't get out of her bed fast enough.

In the next room, the shower continued to run.

"That's it!" Haley muttered crossly, climbing out of bed. "No more Mr. Nice Guy!" Enough was enough! Adam could spend the rest of the morning in the bathroom for all she cared. She was going to have some breakfast!

Pulling on her robe, Haley stormed out to the kitchen where she set the coffee maker in motion, broke some eggs together for an omelet and popped four slices of bread into the toaster oven.

At least there was one kind of hunger she could manage to satisfy without Adam's help, Haley thought irritably as she banged around the kitchen, slamming the cupboard door shut, then dropping the large cast-iron skillet down on top of the stove with a crash. Muttering under her breath, she plopped a pat of butter into the frying pan, then snatched up the mixing bowl and attacked the eggs vigorously with a wire whisk. She had dumped them in on top of the butter and was leaning over with her head stuck in the refrigerator, searching for some cheese, when the sound of approaching footsteps alerted her to the fact that she was no longer alone.

"Good Lord," said Adam, standing in the doorway, "don't you know how to cook anything quiet?"

He winced as she straightened and turned around, slamming the refrigerator door behind her with enough force to make the bottles rattle on their shelves.

"Eggs a little noisy for you, are they?" she said sweetly.

Dammit but he looked good! Even dressed in the previous day's rumpled clothes, his hair still slicked down wet from the shower, a day's growth of beard lining his jaw, he was still the most compellingly attractive man she had ever seen.

"The eggs are fine," Adam said evenly, leaning against the doorjamb. "It's the cook who's giving me a headache."

"Sorry," Haley snapped, not sounding so in the least.

Nuts! she thought, turning her back quite deliberately to check on the progress of the eggs. After what had just happened between them, after he had rejected her without so much as a backward glance, how could she still be feeling that way? She should be angry. She *was* confused. Yet all she could think of at this moment was how much she wanted to go to him, to take him in her arms and hold him tight.

"Just coffee for me," said Adam. He helped himself to a cup, then carried it into the alcove and sat down at the table.

Swearing softly but eloquently, Haley glared at his departing back. She'd gone and cooked all this food and now he had the nerve to say that all he wanted was coffee? Still muttering under her breath, she heaped everything onto her own plate defiantly. Two cheese omelets and four pieces of toast with butter and jelly. It was enough to feed an army!

Affecting an air of total nonchalance, as if she ate that much for breakfast every morning, Haley carried the plate into the alcove, pushed the two typewriters aside and sat down as well.

From across the table, Adam watched as she attacked the food, his expression thoughtful. For a moment, he said nothing, only sipped broodingly at his coffee. Then, apparently, he came to sort some of decision, for he gestured at her overfull plate and asked, "Did—er, anything in particular happen last night to make you work up such an appetite?"

Haley glanced up quickly, too quickly, and a piece of toast lodged in her throat, making her sputter and grab for her glass of juice. Was he serious? she wondered. Did he really not remember what had gone on the night before? She'd never been one to think in terms of revenge, but if the fates were going to hand her the opportunity gift wrapped . . .

Slowly, she cut off another piece of egg, speared it with her fork and placed it in her mouth, chewing the morsel thoroughly before swallowing. "Like what?" she asked finally, her tone deliberately bland.

"You know," Adam hedged, obviously uncomfortable. "Did we—er—did we—?"

"Yes?" Haley prompted, eyes open wide with innocence as she milked the situation to the utmost.

"Damn it, Haley!" Adam growled, setting his coffee cup

down on the table with a thump. "I'm trying to be tactful about this whole thing—the least you could do is help me out. You know what I'm trying to ask!"

Gazing at him mildly, Haley fought hard to suppress a chortle. "Do you mean to say," she asked with just the proper shade of incredulity coloring her tone, *"that you don't remember?"*

Adam frowned as a dull red flush rose over his cheekbones. Then, slowly, he shook his head.

"Ah, well"—Haley sighed dramatically—"how quickly they forget. Another day, another bed; it's all the same—"

"Haley, I'm warning you! I want to know what happened last night, and I want to know now!"

"Tsk tsk tsk," she clucked, shaking her head. "Such impatience. Last night you acted as though you had all the time in the world—"

"HA-LEY!"

"All right," said Haley, pretending to pout. "If you insist. Last night you were the perfect—" she paused, and her eyes danced impishly as she watched the play of emotions over his face and knew he was considering the options"—gentleman!"

"Really?" Adam demanded suspiciously.

Haley's expression now was truly aggrieved. "Would I lie to you?"

"I don't know." Adam stroked his chin thoughtfully. It was clear he still had some unanswered questions. "When I woke up this morning, I wasn't wearing any clothes."

So that was it, thought Haley. No wonder he was confused. Last night when he'd passed out, he'd been holding his drink, and before she'd had a chance to snatch the fallen tumbler from his hand, the liquid had spilled out onto his pants, soaking through to the briefs beneath. At the time, she'd been too bleary-eyed to opt for anything but the easiest course of action. That had been to pull off the wet clothes and drape them over the back of a chair to dry. Indeed, to tell the truth, by that point, she was so far gone that she'd performed the service by rote, scarcely even aware of what she was doing. Not that there was any reason to tell him that, of course.

Spearing another piece of egg, Haley shrugged daintily. "When you have too much to drink, these things happen."

"What things?" Adam growled, his thoughts clearly reverting back to earlier issues.

The giggle, which Haley had been fighting for what seemed like hours, finally erupted. "I tell you, nothing at all went on last night," she gasped out between chortles. "You passed out, and I put you to bed. That's all."

Apparently, her less than serious delivery was not the sort to inspire confidence, for Adam continued to frown at her suspiciously. "I passed out, and you put me to bed," he repeated, as though wanting to make sure he got his facts perfectly straight. "And then we—er, slept?"

"Right." Haley nodded solemnly, but a devilish grin belied her tone.

"I sure as hell don't see what's so funny about all this," Adam muttered crossly, and Haley's giggles erupted anew.

"Maybe you had to be there!" she shrieked gleefully, unable to help herself.

"I *was* there," Adam grated, beginning to lose patience with her rapidly. "That's exactly the problem."

"Oh, I don't know," Haley purred, baiting him deliberately with new doubts. "You didn't seem to mind it at the time."

"Mind *what?*" Adam cried ferociously, a predator pouncing on his prey.

"Why, sleeping," Haley demurred. "Isn't that what we were talking about?"

"I can see I'm not going to get anywhere with you," Adam snapped. Bracing his hands on the table, he rose to his feet and carried his coffee cup into the kitchen.

"That's not what you said last night," Haley murmured with a sly smile.

Adam stopped in his tracks and whirled to face her.

"Just kidding," she cooed.

"I'll be back later to try and get some work done," he announced when he passed by again on his way to the door.

Rising to her feet, Haley followed him across the room. "I'll be ready," she said, standing in the doorway as he walked across the lawn to his car.

"Oh, Adam, one more thing!" Haley called after him suddenly. She didn't expect him to stop, and he didn't. "About last night—you were wonderful!"

The only sign that he had heard was the slight stiffening of his shoulders as Adam climbed into the sports car and slammed the door behind him. Back in the house, Haley collapsed on the couch and laughed until tears ran down her cheeks.

Despite all her intentions to remain calm and rational about the situation, over the next few days, Haley found herself retreating behind a wall of prickly silence. It was bad enough that she'd discovered she was in love with Adam Burke—even worse that he'd chosen that particular moment to reject her, and her advances, outright. Talk about incompatibility!

What she really needed, Haley knew, was time and distance —a chance to sort things through and come to grips with her feelings. Since they were working together so closely, however, both were impossible to come by. Instead, she withdrew. Under the circumstances, it was her only means of self-defense, and she used it, hiding her doubts and confusion behind an attitude of cool indifference. Only then did she feel secure, impervious to Adam's constant assault on her senses.

Despite her uncertainty, Haley found that it was impossible to stay angry with Adam for long, especially when he went out of his way to be so totally endearing. One afternoon she watched with delight as he climbed atop the coffee table and acted out a scene, playing Rex and Allegra both, baritone and soprano alike, until they were finally satisfied with the way it read. How could she help but love a man who would do a silly thing like that?

But the knowledge of her love for Adam brought no solace at all. Indeed, if anything, it made things worse. Her feelings were so clear—now if only she knew what he wanted from her!

Perhaps she shouldn't have taken his rejection quite so seriously, Haley realized. Yet even knowing that she might have misunderstood, the episode still rankled. She would have sworn that he wanted her! And yet . . . the only available evidence strongly suggested that she'd been wrong. In any case, she wasn't about to go fawning all over him again until she had some clear indication of where they stood. She simply wasn't feeling that brave.

This time, the first move would have to be his. If he wanted to make it, fine, she would be there, but there would be no more overtures on her part. No putting herself and her feelings on the line. No, she'd seen where that led, and she was done with it.

Still, her eyes had a way of following Adam as he paced impatiently around the room, blocking out a scene; of watching him as he bent over his typewriter, his long, supple fingers typing out words of love to a dimensionless character who had no use for them. If only, thought Haley, if only just once he would look up from his machine with endearments he'd composed for *her* benefit and not Allegra's! Then she would fly around the table and into his arms in an instant.

Instead, Adam seemed to take his cue from her, and as the week wore on, he began to withdraw, as well. Their conversation grew constrained, their comments brief and to the point, and although they continued to work together as usual, their writing had lost its sparkle, its vitality, and they both knew it.

Eventually, Haley knew, the tension building between them was bound to come to a head. On Friday night, it did.

The week before, T. J. had called to set up a date for an evening of bridge. At the time, it had seemed like a wonderful idea. In the past, the four of them had spent many such pleasant evenings, seated around the card table, challenging each other's skills.

But now, thought Haley, frowning at her reflection in the mirror as she finished buttoning the high-necked Victorian lace blouse she was wearing with her jeans, it was the last thing she felt like doing. In the past two days, she and Adam had regressed to the point where they were barely speaking to one another. Even so, his constant presence was beginning to wear down her will power. Her self-control felt as though it had been stretched almost to the breaking point by the lure of his attraction. It was bad enough she was forced to spend her days with him, Haley thought crossly. Must he now invade her nights as well?

She arrived on the McFarlands' doorstep promptly at the dot of eight, a feat accomplished by setting her watch fifteen minutes ahead, and took inordinate pleasure in the incredulous expression on Adam's face when he arrived and found she'd beaten him there.

"This must be one for the books," he said, settling into the one remaining chair around the card table. "How on earth did you manage it?"

Unwilling to give away any secrets, Haley merely shrugged.

T. J. unfortunately had no such qualms. "She set her watch ahead," she confided. "Isn't that a gas?"

Seated across from her, Dan McFarland shook his head despairingly. "Eighteen years of school behind her and still she talks like she was raised on the streets," he said with a loud sigh.

"Pardon me, dahling," T. J. drawled, lifting her nose in the air. "I meant to say, 'Isn't that just exquisitely amusing?'"

Behind the cover of her hand, Haley snickered loudly.

"No respect," Dan grumbled good-naturedly. "That's what I get around here, no respect."

"That's a husband's lot in life, or didn't you know?" T. J. quipped, smiling at her spouse fondly.

"Funny," said Haley. "I always thought that went the other way around."

"You never know til you try." Adam grinned. Leaning toward Dan, he said in a loud stage whisper, "We should never have let them out of the kitchen in the first place. That's where we went wrong. Now they've gotten the crazy idea that they're as good as we are."

In a mock gesture of empathy for all mankind, they rolled their eyes heavenward.

"Ignore them," said T. J. "That's what I do." She paused, then added devilishly, "And speaking of men who are easy to ignore, what's new with good old Cliff these days?"

"Sheila Downing is," Haley answered quickly, casting a furtive glance at Adam, whose only response was to grin broadly. "I hear they're quite the couple."

"Well, it's about time," T. J. said fervently.

"What's that supposed to mean?" Adam asked with interest.

"I've been telling her for weeks that Cliff was all wrong for her," T. J. said smugly. "Thank God, she's finally seen the error of her ways."

"Oh, I'd say Haley is finished with Cliff, all right." Adam laughed. He paused, then added meaningfully, "All finished."

Out of the corner of her eye, Haley shot him a quick, assessing glance. Surely he wasn't planning to tell them how she'd thrown herself at him, was he? But no, she realized a moment later, that wasn't what Adam had in mind at all. Instead, he was recounting the story of their double date, when Cliff had fallen head over heels for the bounteous and ever-so-willing Sheila.

And as if the story itself wasn't bad enough, T. J. kept interrupting the tale, interjecting pithy comments about the caliber of Haley's taste in men thus far and the necessity of taking her in hand before she did herself any real damage. By the time T. J. had enlisted Adam's aid in the quest of finding the perfect man for Haley, she knew she had heard enough.

"Excuse me," she mumbled, rising quickly to her feet, though not quickly enough to hide her crimson cheeks from the trio seated around her. "I think I'll just go out to the kitchen and help myself to a glass of water."

"Yes, do," Adam agreed, his tone clearly insinuating that she looked as though she could use some cooling off.

"T. J. McFarland, I may never forgive you for this," Haley muttered to herself as she turned on the tap and filled her glass. "Hanging would be too good for you. Burning at the stake, entirely too kind. Maybe drawing and quartering . . ."

"Hey, Haley!" T. J. called from the living room.

Unable to stall much longer, Haley stuck her head around the louvered swinging door.

"Did you hear what Adam just said?" T. J. chortled gleefully.

"No." Haley shook her head. Thank God, she added inwardly.

But T. J. had no intention of sparing her the details. "Come on back in!" she cried, beckoning excitedly with her hand. "Adam says he knows just the man for you!"

"I'll just bet he does," Haley said sweetly, images of Bigfoot flashing through her mind as she took her seat once more.

"No, really!" T. J. said earnestly, turning back to Adam. "Tell us all about him."

"Well," Adam said slowly, as if he needed time to think, "he's tall and dark and handsome. Intelligent, witty and incredibly sexy."

Across the table, Haley's jaw dropped open in surprise. Good Lord! she thought, realizing from the sheepish expression on his face that she couldn't possibly be mistaken. Adam was talking about himself!

"He sounds wonderful." T. J. sighed, her eyes as round as saucers.

"Down, girl." Dan laughed. "You're already spoken for, remember?"

"A girl can dream, can't she?" T. J. shot back sassily.

"Of course, there are a few other character traits that Adam forgot to mention," Haley interjected quickly. "He's also stubborn and unpredictable; and he has definite delusions of grandeur."

"You mean you've already met him?" T. J. squealed.

Haley nodded.

"And you didn't like him?" T. J. made this sound like an impossibility.

"Let's just say he wasn't my type," Haley said pointedly. "Now if you don't mind, can we get on with the game?"

"Sure," Dan said smoothly, picking up the cards and starting to deal.

It was then that Haley realized for the first time that the seating arrangement was all wrong. Dan and T. J. were sitting opposite one another, as were she and Adam, a pairing combination that they never played.

"Hey, wait a minute!" she cried, rising from the table. "We've got to change around here. Adam and I aren't playing as partners."

"Oh, no?" T. J. cocked one eyebrow innocently. "I thought this might be nice for a change."

"Nice?" Haley snapped. "We'll eat each other alive!"

Though she and Adam both played bridge with all the ardor and dedication of true fanatics, it was there that the similarities in their games ended. Each was addicted to a different style of play, and their systems were too radically opposed to one another to ever mesh peaceably. Adam relied on guts and instinct. His bids, Haley knew, often owed more to his intuitive feel of how the play might go than to the cards he was holding in his hand. She, on the other hand, bid with cool, precise logic, scrupulously following the rules that had been set down by the masters. She knew the odds and played them to the hilt.

In the past, she and Adam had never partnered one another. Haley couldn't see any reason why they should start now.

"Come on, be a sport," T. J. cajoled, and Haley looked down at her friend suspiciously. T. J. was up to something; she just knew it! "Surely you wouldn't deny me the pleasure of playing with my own husband just this once?"

"Well . . ." she said slowly. Put like that, there was no way she could refuse, and T. J. knew it. With a small, resigned shrug, she slipped back down into her chair. "I guess just this once won't kill me."

"Great!" T. J. beamed happily.

"Okay, Adam, do your worst," Haley invited. Bracing her elbows on the small table, she leaned toward him with the air of a martyr about to face the lions. "Tell me about these crazy conventions of yours, and I'll try to make some sense out of them."

"Stayman and Blackwood are not crazy," Adam said firmly. "They're useful."

"So is Goren." Haley defended her own system.

"Goren!" Adam snorted derisively. "Nobody plays that anymore!"

"I do," Haley replied huffily. So much for trying to compromise! Maybe she ought to let him try it for a change! "And so will you, if you want to be my partner."

But much to her surprise, Adam immediately backed down. "If you wish," he said silkily, gathering up his cards.

It wasn't until the end of the hand, one in which Dan and T. J. won the bid, then made it, quickly racking up a game on their side of the scoreboard, that Adam spoke up once more, mentioning casually that it was a shame they'd managed to miss finding their fit in spades.

"Now if we'd been bidding my system . . ." His voice trailed away meaningfully, and an eloquent shrug conveyed the rest of the message.

"Oh, all right." Haley sighed, knowing when she was beaten. "Tell me how it goes."

Immediately, Adam's eyes lit up with boyish enthusiasm. "It's a small variation on the Schenken Club—"

"How small?" said Haley, frowning ominously.

Undeterred, Adam held up his hand, the thumb and forefinger spaced no more than an inch apart. "You're going to love it. It's positively ingenious. . . ."

Two hours later, Haley knew with certainty that he'd been wrong. Not only did she not love Adam's bidding system; at the moment, she wasn't too crazy about him, either!

Playing as his partner, Haley found that Adam's bids were quick, decisive and aggressive. Time after time, she found herself being mowed down with no more care than if she'd been a blade of grass standing in the path of a tornado. On the few hands where she'd managed to press her suit successfully and win the bid for her own, he'd laid down his cards as dummy, then come around the table to kibitz behind her shoulder, sucking in his breath sharply in evident dismay each time she reached to play a card. Finally, Haley could stand it no longer.

"That's it!" she cried, slamming down her hand forcibly onto the table. "I refuse to play so much as another card with you peering down over my shoulder like some sort of avenging angel, ready to pounce the moment I make the wrong move."

"What are you talking about?" said Adam, looking some-what taken aback by her outburst. "I'm doing nothing of the sort!"

"Then, pray tell, just what exactly *are* you doing back there?"

"Watching you play the cards, of course," Adam said mildly. "I certainly wasn't trying to give you any cues. In fact," he added self-righteously, "I think I've been a model of self-restraint. No matter how misguided some of your playing's been—"

"Misguided?" Haley cried in outrage.

Unperturbed by the interruption, Adam finished his thought. "—I haven't said so much as a word."

"Maybe not," Haley snapped. "But some of the looks you've been giving me could have melted steel."

"How the hell was I supposed to look when you try to make a slam contract by setting up a cross ruff without even bothering to clear trump first?"

"It worked, didn't it?"

"That's not the point!"

"Oh?" Haley raised one eyebrow mockingly. "Funny, I always thought it was."

"Don't be cute," Adam snapped. "It was a gamble, and you know it. You were damn lucky not to lose everything."

"A calculated gamble," Haley shot back quickly. "And luck had nothing to do with it!" Lord, how her fingers itched to reach out and slap his arrogant face! It was a mistake for the two of them to try and play together; she'd known it from the beginning!

"Really?" Adam drawled. "Are you saying, then, that it was your skill which accounted for the even split in spades?"

"Of course not!" Haley snapped. All the doubts and frustrations of the past few days boiled to the surface, and she gave her anger free rein, knowing full well that the bridge game was not the real issue between them. Knowing but not caring. To be fair, Adam was right. The even split *had* saved her. But at the moment, there was nothing the least bit fair about the way she was feeling. "I was playing the percentages—something a player like you wouldn't know anything about!"

"Ahem!" T. J. cleared her throat loudly. "How about if we break for a cup of coffee?"

"Not for me, thanks," said Haley. Rising to her feet, she shot her friend an apologetic look. "If you don't mind, I think I'd rather just head home. I'm afraid I'm finding the atmosphere here a bit stifling."

"Wait just one minute!" cried Adam.

But Haley never hesitated as she strode quickly across the room, swept her purse off the table in the hall and let herself out the front door. Once outside, she paused on the step, drinking in the cool night air as she allowed the proud set of her shoulders to slump ever so slightly. Then, with a deep, heartfelt sigh, she walked on.

She was halfway across the driveway, eyes downcast as she checked through her purse for her car keys, when the door flew open once more and Adam came dashing out.

"Haley, wait!" he called. He crossed the lawn in three quick strides to catch her elbow and pull her to a stop. "I want to talk to you."

"Well, I most certainly don't want to talk to you!" The quick, backward wrench of her arm accomplished nothing in the way of freedom and plenty in the way of self-inflicted pain. Glaring up at him furiously, Haley resigned herself to listening to what Adam had to say.

"What you did in there was damn rude!"

"Oh, really?" Haley hissed. "And what you did wasn't?" This time, her move must have caught him by surprise, for quite unexpectedly she was free. Turning, she marched away toward her car.

"Oh, no, you don't!"

Haley heard the sound of determined steps behind her and whirled to face him, anger emanating from every pore. The angry words she planned to hurl at him died on her lips, however, as Adam's arm shot out to circle her waist, and she was swept up off her feet and dumped unceremoniously over his shoulder.

"Adam Burke, you put me down this instant!" she demanded furiously, pummeling his back with her balled fists.

"Not on your life!" Adam growled. "You're not running away from me again until we've talked this thing out once and for all." Opening the door to the Zee, he thrust her inside. "No more arguments, Haley. You're coming with me!"

8

~~~~~~~~~~~~~~~~~~~

But my car—" Haley protested faintly.

"Leave it!" Adam grated, climbing in beside her. "It'll be fine here. You can come back for it in the morning."

Of all the arrogant, highhanded men she had ever known, he was clearly the worst! Haley fumed silently. She settled down resignedly in her seat as the Zee backed down the driveway and shot away, tires squealing, down the road. Talk about cave-man tactics—he might as well have bopped her over the head and dragged her home to his den by the hair!

Sneaking a covert look at Adam out of the corner of her eye, Haley sighed. If the grim, set expression on his face was anything to go by, the rest of the evening wasn't going to be any picnic, either!

"All right, out!" Adam ordered several minutes later when they had pulled up in front of the modern glass and wood building that housed his condominium.

Silently, Haley complied. Still without saying a word, she followed him across the walk, up the stairs and in through the front door. Why should she make things any easier for him? she thought defiantly. It was Adam's show, after all. Let him think of something to say!

In the living room, Adam flipped on the light switch, bathing the large area in a soft, muted glow. Quickly, he strode over to the window and pulled the drapes shut. Behind him, Haley remained standing in the arched doorway. She looked around the room, although she'd seen it a thousand times, loving the warm, masculine appeal of its leather and dark wood furniture, the slate fireplace that dominated one wall and the shelves, overflowing with books, that lined two others.

"Now, then," Adam said sternly, breaking into her thoughts. "Suppose you tell me just what that was all about?"

Crossing her arms over her chest, Haley walked forward into the room. "How should I know?" she demanded. "You're the one who started it. I knew it was a mistake for us to ever try and play together!"

Something about the guilty shadow that flickered briefly in Adam's eyes immediately caught Haley's attention. "Oh, no," she groaned, glaring at him accusingly as she guessed the truth. "Don't tell me you set that up?"

"Not at all," Adam disagreed quickly. "It was T. J.'s idea, not mine."

"But you went along with it!"

"Well . . ." Adam hedged. In place of a denial, he offered an excuse. "These last few days have been kind of rough. I thought maybe if we played together, it might help break the ice—although I must admit, this is hardly the result I had in mind."

"What did you expect?" Haley shot back. "First you ruin what was supposed to have been a pleasant evening of bridge—"

"*I* ruined the evening?" Adam repeated incredulously. "Lady, I think you've got a few of your facts backwards. I wasn't the one who threw down my cards and stomped off in a huff like some kindergarten child who's just had her blocks knocked down."

"There you go again!" cried Haley. "Thinking of me like a little kid. Why, you didn't even trust me to play the right cards by myself. And now you have the nerve to wonder why I'm upset!"

"Don't be ridiculous! You're no more of a child than I am."

145

"Well, at least we agree on one thing," Haley snapped. "I was beginning to despair of even that much."

"You?" cried Adam. "How do you think I've felt? This past week has been hell—"

"For both of us," Haley interjected quickly. "You're not the only one who's been having a tough time of it, you know."

"No, I don't know," said Adam, his voice suddenly soft, persuasive. "Suppose you tell me about it."

For a moment, Haley hesitated, opposing impulses warring within her. Did she dare tell him how she felt? Did she dare leave herself open like that, without first having some sign that her feelings, her needs, her desires, were reciprocated?

"Come on, kid. Whatever it is that's bothering you can't be all that bad." Drawing her forward, Adam pushed her down gently onto the plush couch. "Why don't you just sit right down here and tell me all about it?"

Perhaps it was the calm assurance in his tone, the complacent male confidence that she would automatically accede to his wishes, that immediately set off warning bells in Haley's head. He sounded so sure of himself, she thought. And yet, in some ways, not at all like the Adam she knew. She'd heard those words somewhere before, hadn't she . . . ?

Biting her lower lip, Haley frowned, trying to remember. Then, all at once, it came to her. Gulping uneasily, she almost wished it hadn't. Those were Rex's words. He'd used them in a similar situation two chapter earlier. Adam had written the scene himself; she remembered that now. Well, the soft, honeyed approach may have worked on Allegra, but she was damned if it was going to do the same for her!

"Stop pushing me around!" she snapped, bouncing back up off the couch to stand before him. "I am not Allegra!"

But if Haley had expected an explosion in return, she was in for a surprise. Instead, Adam merely sank down into the seat she had vacated, relaxing back against the plump cushions and leaning his arm casually along the upper ridge of the couch. "Thank God for that," he muttered.

"What's that supposed to mean?" Haley demanded, gazing down at him suspiciously.

He looked so comfortable stretched out on the sofa that all at once she felt rather foolish asserting her independence by towering above him. Stiffly, she sat down as well, and immediately Adam's arm reached out to circle her shoulders and draw her close. Ignoring Haley's token protest, he nestled her body next to his.

"That's better," Adam murmured, his breath warm on the top of her head; and although Haley wanted to argue, to stay angry with him, she somehow found herself relaxing against his shoulder and nodding in agreement.

Still, she thought, no matter how mellow she was suddenly feeling, there was one question she wanted answered. "Now suppose you explain what that crack you made was all about?"

"I would think you already knew the answer to that," Adam said softly. "Haven't you realized yet that Allegra is not my type?"

"Oh, no?" Surprised, Haley drew back her head and looked up at him searchingly. "Why not?"

Unexpectedly, Adam grinned. "Not enough fight in that one," he said affably. "Why, she lets Rex walk all over her."

"Is that so?" All of a sudden, Haley was feeling better, more lighthearted than she had in days. She'd wanted Adam to make the first move, and now, looking at things calmly and rationally, she could see that he had done just that by dragging her back to his home to talk things out. So what if his methods left something to be desired? She certainly couldn't fault his intentions! Suddenly, Haley couldn't wait to meet Adam half-way.

Leering up at him playfully, she purred in her sexiest voice. "Are you saying you wouldn't like to walk all over me?"

Still grinning, Adam shook his head. "No, I don't think so. Anyhow, it's a moot point because I sure as hell know better than to try!"

"Really?" Haley said teasingly. "I'm glad to hear that our time together has taught you a few things."

"Actually, I know lots of things," Adam said softly, his lascivious wink leaving little doubt as to what direction his thoughts were taking. "Would you like to try some of them out?"

"That depends." Pausing, Haley pretended to consider the offer. "They don't involve any Hobie Cats, do they?"

"Not a catamaran in sight," Adam confirmed, and she felt his chest vibrate with silent laughter.

"In that case," she murmured throatily, "you're the boss."

Haley reached up to run her finger tip along the chiseled line of Adam's jaw, but to her surprise, he jerked away as though he had been stung. Grasping her shoulders, he set her stiffly away, then rose to his feet and strode across the room, one hand massaging the back of his neck in obvious agitation.

"What's the matter?" Haley asked in bewilderment, rising to follow him. "Adam, where are you going?"

As she came up behind him, Adam spun on his heel. "Why did you say that?" he demanded, his voice tight.

"Say what?" Haley was now thoroughly confused. What on earth could have set him off like this?

"You called me the boss," Adam said, slowly and distinctly. "Now what did you mean by that?"

"Nothing," cried Haley, shrugging perplexedly. "Nothing at all. It was just—"

"Just what?"

Good God, thought Haley, what was this, the Spanish Inquisition? He was a fine one to go around questioning what she chose to call him. To tell the truth, she hadn't even really been aware that she'd adopted the nickname, but now, especially when he was in a temper such as this, it certainly seemed appropriate!

"Maybe it had something to do with this need you seem to have to constantly be in charge!" she snapped, sighing inwardly. So much for detente. The moment she thought she had him all figured out, why did he have to go and turn everything upside down all over again?

"Are you saying I'm domineering?"

"Not at all!" Haley retorted, growing angrier by the moment. "What I'm really saying is that you're a stubborn, pig-headed oaf! And if you can't recognize what was supposed to have been an endearment when you hear one, then I'm not about to try and explain it to you, because at the moment I'm rather hard pressed to remember why I should ever want to say anything nice to you at all!"

"An endearment?" Adam said skeptically. "Is that what you think that is?"

"Well, by all means, if you disagree, let's do something about it," Haley said sarcastically, remembering the choices he had given her. "Now, then, which would you prefer—sugar? Darling?" She paused and glared at him furiously. "How about babycakes?"

"Babycakes?" Adam roared. Then, abruptly, his features softened. "Babycakes?" he repeated incredulously, the beginnings of a smile playing about his lips.

"All right." Haley shrugged haughtily, refusing to be placated. "Frankly, I think it sounds a little silly, but if that's what you want—"

"Oh, God, Haley, come here, would you?" Adam groaned, hauling her into his arms. "What are we doing to each other?" His hand came up to stroke her hair, his fingers tangling in the silky strands as he tucked them away behind her ear. "Why are we arguing like this? It's madness," he murmured softly, the words barely audible. "I don't want to fight with you. I want to make love with you."

Bracing her hands against his shoulders, Haley pushed away, her dark eyes finding and holding his. "Why the hell didn't you say so?" she demanded crossly. "I'm not a mind reader, you know."

Though he tried his best to look stern, Adam's lips twitched with poorly suppressed amusement. "I've been trying my best

149

not to rush you, woman. I had to make sure that you wanted this every bit as much as I did."

"Is that why you got so upset when I said you were the boss?" Haley mused aloud, filled with sudden insight.

Above her, Adam nodded. "The last thing I needed was for you to start humoring me. But what else was I to think? You've spent the past week treating me as though I were the lowest form of life. Tell me about it," he said earnestly. "Tell me what's wrong. Did I do something really awful to you Monday night? I've tried and tried, but I swear, I just can't remember."

"Oh, Adam," Haley moaned, swamped by feelings of guilt. "You didn't do anything wrong. In fact, to tell the truth, you weren't in any shape to do anything at all. You won the last hand, then passed out before you could claim the prize."

"Talk about poor timing!" Adam muttered disgustedly. His lips came down to feather a kiss softly on her forehead, followed by another on her cheek, then yet another on the tip of her nose. "I don't suppose by any chance that the offer is still open?"

"Oh, no." Haley shook her head solemnly, but the hand that circled his waist tugged the cotton shirt free of his pants, her fingers dipping provocatively beneath it to caress the satiny warmth of his skin. "I'm afraid that was a one-shot deal, take it or leave it."

"I see," said Adam. He paused as if considering his options. "In that case, I guess I have no choice but to play the stubborn, pig-headed oaf and take charge of the situation!"

Before Haley could realize what he had in mind, she found herself being swept up off her feet for the second time that evening. This time, however, she was cradled gently in Adam's arms, her body held close against the wall of his chest as he strode purposefully across the room, then down the hall to his bedroom.

Once there, Adam lowered her to her feet once more, her body sliding sensuously down the length of his until she stood before him. With a muffled groan of desire, he pulled her forward into his embrace. Cupping her face with his hands, Adam tilted her head back, then lowered his own until the final short distance separating them was gone, obliterated by the touch of his lips on hers. The pressure of his mouth was gentle at first, and Haley's eyelids slid shut. She leaned into his body, the strength suddenly seeming to have vanished from her own. Their mouths were warm and wet as they moved together, tongues finding each other, then circling sensuously, engaged in a mating dance whose intensity rocked them both.

Haley's heart hammered in her breast as Adam's hands slid down along her sides, arching her body into his. Their hips ground together, and she felt his taut strength, proof of his arousal, which in turn served to heighten her own. Then she was moving with him, her hips writhing sinuously in time with his. Adam's tongue plunged deep within the honeyed well of her mouth, withdrew, then plunged again, and Haley's senses reeled at this foreshadowing of pleasures to come.

Adam's hands slid downward into the back pockets of her blue jeans, his fingers cupping and kneading the soft flesh of her buttocks. His lips did not release hers as he used this new hold to walk her slowly across the room. The muscles of his thighs strained against the taut denim of his jeans as he guided her with utmost care. Step by step, they moved closer and closer to the large double bed.

Then he was lowering her gently down onto the coverlet. There was a moment's hesitation as he knelt and removed her shoes, tossing the flimsy sandals carelessly away over his shoulder. His hands moved tenderly over her naked feet, his fingers caressing her toes, her instep, then her ankles before slipping beneath the hem of her jeans to glide upward over the smooth skin of her calves.

It was torture, thought Haley, feeling as though she were about to die with the waiting, the wanting. She gasped as his hands slipped away, then returned, moving outside her narrow, straight-legged pants, stroking upward over her knees and then her thighs. The path made by his fingers seemed to burn into her flesh, even through the thick denim that still separated them.

Kneeling between her legs, Adam let his hands move slowly upward, his palms following the taut muscles of her upper thighs, his fingers shaping her legs and holding them apart. His thumbs trailed carelessly along the inner seam of her pants until they met at the juncture of her legs and pressed firmly, igniting the sensitive flesh beneath.

"Adam, please!" Haley gasped, reaching down to pull him to her.

But Adam refused to be hurried. "All in good time," he murmured, bending low so that his lips could follow the trail his hands had blazed.

Her head tossing restlessly from side to side, Haley twisted beneath him. How had he managed to bring her to this fever pitch so quickly? she wondered dazedly. They hadn't even removed so much as one article of clothing, yet already her heart was beating violently, her blood pounding in her veins, her body suffused with a fiery flood of liquid heat. Never before had she been so aroused, so attuned to every nerve ending her body possessed.

"Damn you, Adam Burke," she whispered, quivering violently as his lips came down to kiss the hard knot of material where the two seams joined just below the zipper of her pants. Tilting his head back, Adam inhaled deeply, smiling at her impatience.

"What's your hurry?" he murmured, mocking her gently. "We've got all night."

"Easy for you to say," Haley growled. She sighed as he moved finally up alongside of her, her hands reaching out to him feverishly. "Oh, Adam, I'm not sure I can wait much longer!"

Slipping her hands beneath his shirt, Haley's fingers splayed out over the smooth muscles of his back as their mouths found each other once more, fusing them together in a kiss whose demanding passion sent them spiraling on to new heights of desire. Grasping the hem in impatient fingers, she drew the shirt upward and off over Adam's head, then tossed it away.

Finally, then, his hands were moving to undress her as well. Adam's fingers brushed lightly over the high lace collar of her ruffled blouse, seeking the row of tiny buttons that held it shut.

"Good Lord," he muttered irreverently several moments later, his voice muffled by the pressure of his mouth against her own. Making only minimal progress, his fingers stumbled impatiently over the myriad buttons. Drawing back his head, he gazed down at the row of fasteners and groaned raggedly. "This blouse is worse than Chinese water torture!"

"Would you like some help?" asked Haley, the ghost of a smile beginning to play about her lips.

Frowning in concentration, Adam ignored her question. "It never happens like this in those romance novels," he grumbled under his breath, and Haley's smile blossomed full force. "There the hero unfastens one button, and the next thing you know, she's naked to the waist."

Finally, the last button slipped through its hole. Breathing a sigh of evident relief, Adam smoothed the edges of the blouse aside, only to be confronted by the sight of the white satin camisole she wore beneath it.

"Don't tell me there's more," he groaned, glaring down at this new obstacle with all the warmth of a dripping icicle. Then he looked up, and the glare was transferred to her instead. "I swear, Haley Morgan, I've about reached the end of my rope with you!"

His expression was so engagingly wistful, so endearingly boyish, that for a moment, Haley forgot her own impatience, forgot that she, too, was anxious for what was to come. Her frustration vanished, replaced instead by a surge of overwhelming tenderness. In a sudden flash of insight, she realized that never before had she known such happiness—such complete and total joy. Perhaps it was her upbringing that had been responsible for the notion that sex was serious business, but certainly she'd never seen that fact disputed before. Yet all at once, Haley knew that with Adam it would be different—that they would laugh as freely as they loved, that their coming together would not be a solemn ritual of well-measured give-and-take, rather a joyous celebration of the best that life had to offer.

"Don't worry," she said softly, aglow with these new and unfamiliar feelings. "This one's much easier than it looks. It just slips off over my head."

"Thank God for that!" Adam growled crossly, and suddenly Haley could contain her giggles no longer.

Drawing back, Adam gazed down at her incredulously. "Laugh at me, will you? You'll get yours!"

"Well, I should hope so," Haley said lightly. She leaned forward so that he could pull the camisole off, then smiled up at him impishly. "And after all this time, it had better be good!"

"It will be," Adam promised fervently, the warmth of his gaze washing over her reverently. "Believe me, Haley, it will be."

It was only a moment until the remaining clothing that separated them was disposed of as well; then they lay together naked, wrapped in each other's arms. Glorying in the feel of flesh against flesh, they explored each other's bodies for the first time. Tentatively at first and then with more abandon, they pleasured each other with touches—brushing, stroking, finding those tender spots whose caress brought an immediate gasp of delight to their half-parted lips.

As if she could never get enough, Haley's hands roamed freely over Adam's body, caressing from shoulder to thigh and reveling in the shuddering intensity of his response. Pushing his body down onto the yielding mattress, she sprawled luxuriously on top of him, her hair falling forward over her shoulder and covering his chest like a heavy silken veil as she brushed her tongue delicately along the hollow of his throat. Sliding sensuously downward, she teased and tantalized with her touch, her fingers seeking through the curling mat of hair until they found the flat nipples and caressed them to hardness. Then her tongue followed, and her mouth closed over the bud. Rolling it between her lips, she sucked on it deeply.

Adam groaned beneath her, his breathing deep and uneven. Haley could feel the surging beat of his heart beneath the palm that nestled against his hair-roughened chest. Dipping lower, she explored the contours of his body fully, her warm hands seeking, finding. Firmly, she stroked his velvet smoothness, delighting in the evidence of his desire.

"Haley," Adam moaned, her name a whispered incantation.

Then she gasped in surprise as suddenly he took charge, grasping her shoulders and rolling over to trap her beneath him. It was Adam's turn to be the aggressor. His palms shaped her breasts, kneading them gently. Pushing her head back into the pillow, Haley arched her body upward convulsively, seeking his touch.

"Yes," she whispered, sighing, and his knowing hands slipped lower. She sucked in her breath sharply, wanting, needing the intimacy of his caress. Adam's touch was pure magic as he aroused her further still, his fingers stroking with a sure, steady rhythm that transported her to a paradise where time and place no longer existed, where nothing mattered save pleasure and sensation and the devastating needs he evoked within her.

"Now, Adam," she whispered. "Please . . ."

Then he was there. Parting her legs gently, he slipped between them. Gracefully, easily, he took her and made them one.

Their lovemaking was wild and primitive as they came together for the first time, a surging torrent of unleashed desire that overwhelmed them both. Haley felt her body tightening with a tension that demanded its own release, her limbs tingling with a heat that spread slowly inward until her entire body throbbed with the pulsating rhythm. Then the knot coiling within her exploded, and she fell over the edge of the world and carried Adam with her, their bodies clasped together in a shuddering, satisfying climax.

It was a moment before either was able to speak. His elbows resting on either side of her head, Adam slumped languidly over her. Equally drained, Haley rested beneath him, devastated by an experience that had surpassed all expectation. What they had shared was something special, even rare, and they both knew it.

"Wow," Haley said softly as Adam rolled to one side, then reached down to pull the sheet up over them.

Gazing down at her warmly, Adam smiled. "I know what you mean."

Flinging her hands up over her head, Haley stretched with feline grace. "I think we've given the words earth shattering a whole new context."

Leaning up on his side, Adam braced up on his elbow, his head resting in one hand, the other toying idly with the thick strands of black hair that fanned about the pillow in careless disarray. "I knew we'd be good together," he murmured. "God, Haley, it seems as though I've wanted you forever."

At that, Haley's eyes flew open wide, jolted down to her toes by his confession. "You?" she sputtered, sitting up with a jerk. Grasping his shoulders, she shoved him down onto the mattress, then hovered above him, shaking her finger in his face accusingly. "You're a fine one to talk. I've been waiting seven years for you to come to your senses!"

"Damn!" Adam swore. Snapping his fingers, he grinned up at her wolfishly. "I never thought of that."

"What?" asked Haley, now thoroughly confused.

"Seven years," Adam muttered, shaking his head sadly. "Do you suppose that's all this is—the seven-year itch?"

"You dope!" Haley cried, laughing. Picking up her pillow, she dropped it over his face. "You've got it all backwards."

"Who, me?" One eye and just the tip of a delicately arched brow peeked out from behind the pillow.

"Of course. Don't you see? After seven years with me, you're supposed to be out scratching somewhere else."

"Oh, well," Adam sighed. Brushing the pillow aside, he swung his feet over the side of the bed and started to rise. "If you insist."

"Don't you dare!" Catching him neatly about the waist, Haley pulled him, unresisting, back to her side. "Don't you know it's bad luck to change beds in the middle of the night?"

"That's funny," Adam said teasingly. "I always thought that proverb had something to do with horses midstream."

"Whatever," she agreed blithely, waving her hand in the air. "In any case, consider yourself taken."

"Taken, am I?" Adam growled with mock ferocity. "You've got your nerve! In fact," he commented, gazing at her thoughtfully, "considering your behavior over the past few days, I think you're probably damn lucky I made love with you at all! You've been impossible, you know. Don't try to deny it."

"I won't if you won't!" Haley shot back spiritedly. "You were no bed of roses yourself! Besides, I had every reason to be angry with you."

"Oh?" Adam's butter-wouldn't-melt-in-my-mouth expression clearly conveyed his feeling that he had done no wrong.

"Let's just say I'm not very good at handling rejection," Haley said softly, her eyes clouding over at the memory. "And as I recall, you didn't even have the decency to try and soften the blow. You just turned your back and ran!"

"Have some pity, woman!" Adam cried. "As *I* recall, I was in pain."

"You told me you were fine."

"And you believed me?" Adam asked incredulously. "Hell, I was bellowing like a bull elephant with a thorn in its foot!"

Grinning cheekily, Haley shrugged. "For all I know, you might sound that way every morning when you wake up."

At that, Adam smiled as well. "Tomorrow you'll have a chance to find out."

"Will I?" Haley murmured. Snuggling in beside him, she

nestled into the curve of his shoulder, and Adam's arm closed over her protectively, cuddling her close against his side.

"You most certainly will," he whispered.

For a long moment, there was only silence between them. Haley relaxed and let her thoughts drift, immersed in a peace more profound than any she had known before. This was where she was meant to be—here in Adam's arms, where she had found the sort of happiness she thought only existed in her dreams.

The love she felt for him swelled within her breast, filling her with an emotion so fierce that for a moment Haley could only catch her breath at the wonder of it all. They belonged together, she and Adam—two of a kind, partners in work, and now, partners in love.

When Adam spoke again, his words were slow, thoughtful. "Do you want to know what I was really thinking that morning when you told me that I had lost the bet?" he asked softly.

Drawing back her head, Haley leaned up on one elbow and nodded.

Remembering, Adam smiled. "I had just woken up in your bed, and I was thinking that if that was the sort of treatment the loser got, then winning must have been sheer heaven."

"Mmmm," Haley purred contentedly. Her hand reached up to trace the line of his jaw. "I couldn't agree with you more."

"I was hoping you might feel that way."

"Any particular reason?" Haley inquired archly.

"Actually, I had in mind trying to create that particular slice of heaven again."

"Already?" Haley gulped in surprise.

"Too soon?" Adam said blandly, the corners of his eyes crinkling with amusement.

"No—not for me," Haley stammered. "But I always thought—"

"Yes?"

Dammit, he wasn't going to help her at all, was he? Grinning wickedly, she let her hand slip downward, her fingers running lightly, teasingly, over his stomach. "I'm ready," she said huskily. "But I thought men were the ones who got into technical difficulty at times like this."

"Ahem!" Adam cleared his throat loudly. "Are you implying that I might be over the hill?" He leered down at her cheerfully as his body's immediate response to her touch rapidly belied his words.

"Not me, boss." Haley shook her head meekly.

"You know," Adam drawled, "now that I think about it, I'll bet I could grow to like that name." Capturing her wandering hand in one of his own, he rolled quickly, letting his full weight descend on her and crushing her down into the soft mattress. "At times like this, it makes me feel positively feudal."

"Really?" Haley gazed up at him, her dark eyes open wide with innocence. Then, unable to help herself, she ruined that image by wriggling beneath him suggestively. "Does that mean you want to play master and serving girl?"

"Try me . . ." Adam invited huskily, and it was hours later, when the first streaks of dawn's light had already appeared across the horizon, before they fell into a deep, dreamless sleep, cradled in the loving embrace of each other's arms.

If Haley could have envisioned what the perfect life would be like, the next two weeks would have come close. It was a time of laughter and of joy, of living and loving in total harmony. No longer did she question now or why. For the time being, it was enough that she and Adam had each other. That was all that mattered. Day and night, they were inseparable, working and playing with equal fervor as the creative juices began to flow once more and they produced chapter after chapter of polished prose, words flowing effortlessly between them.

"So after all this time, we've finally brought them full circle," Haley observed one afternoon. Sitting behind her typewriter, her fingers hovered expectantly over the keys. "Rex and

Allegra are back in the airport where they were supposed to have been when the story opened. Now that they've arrived home, what do you suppose we ought to have them do next?"

"I know what I'd like to do next," Adam said meaningfully, coming up to stand behind her. He rested his hands on her shoulders, massaging them lightly.

"I'll just bet you do." Haley laughed, flexing her muscles languidly beneath his hands. "But there is a small matter of work that needs to be done."

"Later," Adam whispered. He leaned down to draw the tip of his tongue around the edge of her ear in a tantalizing caress. Slowly, his hands slid downward until they cupped her breasts, full and swollen in his palms. "I'm afraid Rex and Allegra will just have to wait their turn."

"But—" Then the protest was gone, lost in a gasp of pleasure as Adam slipped one finger inside her shirt, swirling it into the small indentation of her navel. "Mmm, that feels wonderful . . ." With a sigh, Haley tipped her head back against the top of the chair, abandoning herself to the erotic sensations evoked by his touch.

Then, abruptly, she straightened back up, her eyes alight with discovery. "That's it!" she cried delightedly.

"That's what?" asked Adam, perplexed by her sudden withdrawal.

"The next scene! We'll have Rex try that on Allegra—she'll love it!"

"I'm sure she will," Adam commented dryly.

"No, really!" Haley enthused, fitting her fingers to the keyboard once more. "Now let me see—what exactly were you doing? Where did you have your hands?"

"Why don't I show you?" Adam offered ingenuously, beginning to do just that. "Then you can see for yourself exactly where everything goes."

"Adam," Haley protested faintly as his fingers moved slowly down the buttons of her blouse. "If you keep that up much longer, I won't be in any shape for taking notes."

Reaching over her shoulder, Adam flipped the switch on her machine, and it immediately fell silent. "That's exactly what I was hoping for," he murmured huskily, applying himself to the task until Rex and Allegra were the farthest thing from Haley's mind . . .

But if the days were good, the nights were even better—long, hot summer nights spent learning the language of each other's bodies and the tenor of their own needs and desires.

Friends and lovers, Haley thought happily. That's what they were. A rare and multifaceted relationship that offered much more fulfillment than she would ever have dreamed possible. Life was perfect—everything she could have asked for and more. So why, then, did she have this vague feeling of unrest—this nagging sixth sense that told her that such bliss couldn't possibly last?

Was this time a magic interlude? she wondered. Was it a golden opportunity for them to forge a bond for the future? Or was it merely a fantasy world of her own making—a one-way ticket to disillusion and disaster?

Drawing a deep, uncertain breath, Haley sighed. Only time would tell.

9

By the end of the following week, *Passionate Strangers* was finished.

With a yelp of sheer delight, Haley typed in the final sentence, then tore the sheet from her typewriter. "Good-by, Rex and Allegra," she intoned, laying the page atop the pile dramatically. "May you rest in peace."

"What a somber attitude you have." Adam chided her with a smile. "Are you sure you don't mean, may you live happily ever after?"

"That, too," Haley declared breezily. Leaning back, she stretched her arms high above her head, fingers reaching toward the ceiling. "Lord, what a relief! I have to admit there were times when I doubted we'd ever get it done."

"Me, too," Adam agreed. He rose from his chair and walked around the table. Leaning down over her shoulder, he looked at the completed manuscript with satisfaction.

"I'm glad to see you've found your proper place at last," Haley quipped. She grinned at Adam's quizzical expression. "You know what they say—behind every great woman stands a man!"

"So that's all I am to you, is it?" Adam shook his head ruefully. "The little man who made it all possible?"

Haley shrugged modestly. "I have to admit, I couldn't have done it without you."

"Nor I, you. We make a great team, don't we, kid?" Adam sketched his hands through the air as if picturing the words printed on a marquee. "Burke and Morgan—Purveyors of Romance, Fulfillers of Fantasy!"

"Yes," Haley agreed slowly, thoughtfully. "We certainly do."

But later that night, long after Adam had fallen asleep, his deep, even breathing sounding a steady cadence at her side, his teasing words came back to haunt her, and Haley found she could not sleep at all.

Now what? she wondered uneasily as all the doubts she'd spent the past few weeks suppressing came winging their way back to the surface. Where did she and Adam go from there? The book, the romance, which had bound them so irrevocably together, was finished. That shared intensity of purpose, that sense of commitment to a common goal, was gone. Would their own romance now begin to dissipate as well?

Mashing her pillow into a large, lumpy ball, Haley crossed her arms on top of it and rested her chin in her hands. A team, that's what Adam had called them. And they were—a team of accomplished writers. Had she been deluding herself to think that they were something more?

Frowning uneasily, Haley remembered Adam's next words— "Purveyors of Romance, Fulfillers of Fantasy." What an odd choice of phrase! Then, with a sudden, uncomfortable gulp, she recalled one of the first conversations she and Adam had had about the book. At the time, he had chided her for not believing in romance. Could it be that he had set out deliberately to do something about that—to supply the romance that up till that point had been so conspicuously absent from her life? What if the whole interlude had been nothing more than a sham, a way of keeping her happy, of ensuring that she would remain in the right frame of mind, a romantic frame of mind, until the all-important manuscript was finished?

Adam Burke—purveyor of romance, fulfiller of fantasies . . . Adam Burke, prime louse! Haley thought furiously, quelling a sudden urge to reach out and punch him right in the nose. He looked so innocent in sleep, she mused. Could he really have hatched such a scheme? He couldn't be that rotten, could he?

Vainly, Haley searched through her memory, replaying the last ten days of idyllic pleasure in her mind. No, she realized, he had never once mentioned the future or a commitment of any kind. Certainly neither of them had spoken anything of love. She for all the obvious reasons. And Adam's reason could have been equally obvious. Perhaps he hadn't spoken any words of love because there'd been none to say.

Then, abruptly, an idea began to take root in her mind. A small glimmer of hope that Haley nurtured with all the enthusiasm of the truly desperate. Just because Adam didn't love her now didn't mean that the situation couldn't be remedied with time. Why on earth should she give up just because the book was over and done? There would always be another idea, another book to write. And, in the meantime, she and Adam would still be together.

No, there was no reason to panic, Haley decided, feeling suddenly much better. This script wasn't finished yet by a long shot. There were still several very important scenes she had yet to write. But for now, all she really had to do was bide her time.

That weekend, Dan and T. J. had planned to invite a few friends over for a barbecue in their back yard. Ever the inveterate hostess, however, T. J. loved nothing better than a good party, and on hearing of the completion of Adam and Haley's book, she pounced on it as the excuse she needed to broaden the guest list and turned the event into a celebration bash.

Not much of a party goer by nature, Haley was the first to admit that she would have vastly preferred the first plan—a quiet evening with Adam and the McFarlands, and perhaps a few other close friends for company. But Adam was persuasive and T. J. adamant, and in the end, she found herself giving in gracefully. Indeed, by the time Saturday night rolled around, she was even beginning to look forward to what promised to be a boisterous affair.

After showering and washing her hair, Haley dressed with care. Though she and Adam had gone many places together in the past, it would be their first public appearance as a couple, and she wanted him to be proud of her.

Looking through the selection of dresses in her closet, she chose a strapless sun dress made out of delicate white gauze. The shirred bodice held the dress securely in place over her small, high breasts, while the full skirt rustled sensuously about her slim legs. The filmy material covered her with the teasing transparency of a gossamer cobweb, mandating the flesh-colored body stocking she wore underneath. Twirling in front of the mirror, Haley was pleased to note that the dress's creamy color set off her dark golden tan to perfection. To that, she added only a pair of white high-heeled sandals and small pearl stud earrings, creating an effect that was casual, yet elegant in its simplicity.

Remembering Adam's displeasure with her curls, she let her hair dry naturally. It hung like a thick black veil, long and sleek and gleaming, down the center of her back; and Adam's wolf whistle of appreciation when she greeted him at the door was more than ample reward for the efforts she had made.

"Has anyone told you yet today that you're beautiful?" he murmured, drawing her into his arms for a hug.

"Let me see," Haley said teasingly, pretending to think. "There was the mailman, and the gas station attendant, and then the deli-man at the supermarket . . ."

"The worst thing is, I believe you," Adam growled, nuzzling her neck suggestively. "Are you sure we have to go to this party? In that outfit, I'm not at all sure I want to offer you up for public consumption."

Straightening, Haley pulled away. "You were the one who was wildly enthusiastic about all this, not me," she pointed out mildly. "But now that T. J. has set us up as the guests of honor, don't you think it would be rather rude of us not to appear?"

"I suppose so." Adam shrugged. Unexpectedly, he reached out and hooked one finger behind the top edge of her bodice, pulling it out away from her body so that he could lean down and glance inside.

"Hey!" cried Haley, slapping his hand away. "What do you think you're doing?"

"Just checking." Adam grinned unrepentantly. "That's some dress you're wearing. Before I risk losing you to the clamoring hordes, I wanted to make damn sure you're wearing more underneath there than meets the eye!"

Laughing at his outrageous behavior, Haley linked her arm through his and led the way to the car. The drive to the McFarlands' house took only a matter of moments. To Adam's delight and Haley's consternation, they were able to hear the first strains of music from the band T. J. had hired at the last moment from over a block away, while the only parking space they were able to find on the sunny residential street involved a full five-minute walk before they even reached the house.

"Come on in!" cried T. J., throwing open the front door. "It's about time the guests of honor got here!"

Haley allowed herself to be ushered inside, then followed along behind as T. J. led the way through the house and out onto the patio overlooking the large back yard.

Seeing the vast throng of people already assembled there, Haley's eyes opened wide with shock. "Wow, what a bash!" She laughed nervously. "Did you send out invitations to this party, or did you just take a billboard in downtown Greenwich that said, 'Come one, come all'?"

"Now, now." T. J. patted her arm reassuringly. "It isn't really as bad as it looks. So there's a bit of a crowd—you know how these things have a way of getting out of hand."

"Out of hand?" Haley cried, gesturing at the assemblage. "That's putting it mildly. In case you haven't noticed, this one's not only out of hand, it's out of house and out of yard!"

"Shhh," T. J. whispered. "Don't let Dan hear you say that.

He got a little upset when he saw the town softball team arrive, but I think he's finally beginning to get over it. The last thing I need is for something to set him off again. Besides," she added blithely, "I've found that crowds this size are only dangerous when they're hungry. And I intend to see that the beer keeps flowing, the punch is well spiked, and everybody's well fed. What could possibly go wrong?"

What indeed? Haley wondered as she found herself being drawn forward into the throng. Almost immediately, she was surrounded by a group of wellwishers, friends with whom she had temporarily lost touch while she and Adam buried themselves in their work. It was always like that when they were writing, and anyone who knew them well understood. While a book was in progress, they worked to the exclusion of practically all else. Then, when it was finished, they sprang forth once more, suddenly freed and ready to live like normal people until the next idea overtook them.

"Haley, how've you been? It's been ages . . ."

Engulfed by a crowd of boisterous friends, Haley threw herself into the spirit of the party wholeheartedly. Though she started at Adam's side, it wasn't long before the hand that had grasped his tightly held a drink instead as they drifted farther and farther apart, each claimed by a new circle of revelers.

"Hey, Morgan, I hear you're into romance these days. I don't suppose there's any way I can capitalize on that, is there?" Jeff Phillips was a good friends of Dan's. He was also an incorrigible rake who flirted shamelessly with any and all women, single or otherwise. Now he leered down at her playfully, his question a teasing reference to the time she had fixed a leak in his pipes after researching their book on plumbing.

"I don't think so, Jeff," Haley bantered back with a laugh. "Not this time."

"Oh, well." He shrugged good-naturedly. "At least you've got to give a guy points for trying."

Grinning, Haley favored him with a knowing look. "So now

you're working on a point system, eh? With your record, I always did wonder how you managed to keep track of the score!"

To his credit, Jeff managed a sheepish grin. "I always knew you were quick on your feet, Haley, love," he said admiringly. "But that's hitting below the belt."

"You said it, not me," Haley agreed gaily, and the two of them laughed together.

"Well, then," said Jeff, "now that we both know where we stand, how about a dance?"

"Well . . ." Haley hedged, looking about quickly over his shoulder. Where was Adam, anyway? "Maybe just one."

It wasn't until they'd reached the dance floor that she finally spotted him, standing off to one side in a large group of people. Mostly women, Haley noted cattily, and all of them hanging on his every word. Damn Adam Burke, anyway! While she was stuck there dancing with some latter-day Casanova, he was out having the time of his life, spreading around his not inconsiderable charm.

Mutinously, she glared at Adam over Jeff's broad shoulder, daring him to turn around. The least he could do was have the decency to look jealous! she decided, fuming inwardly. But when Adam finally did notice, as she and Jeff danced by, he simply smiled and waved, a small, almost impersonal gesture that did nothing to acknowledge the fact that her partner's hands had tightened about her waist until she felt as though the two of them had been welded together.

What was the matter with Adam, anyway? Haley wondered crossly, irritated that she couldn't spark even the tiniest show of possessive behavior. Was he really so uninvolved that he didn't care?

As soon as the dance was over, Haley disengaged herself quickly, but by the time she reached the spot where she had last seen Adam, he had disappeared once more. Really! she thought indignantly, quelling a childish urge to stamp her foot in frustration. She'd be damned if she was going to spend the night running around after him as if they were engaged in some demented game of hide-and-seek. From now on, if Adam wondered what she was up to, he could come and find her!

Dan was the next to claim her attention. Grabbing her hand and dragging her over to the mammoth brick barbecue pit, he insisted that no party was complete without a sample of his delicious home cooking. Haley's laughing protests went for naught as he piled her plate high with a thick hamburger on a hard roll, potato salad and two fat dill pickles.

"Stop!" she cried, watching incredulously as he reached for a hot dog to add to the pile. "I'll never be able to eat all that as it is!"

"Really?" Dan appeared genuinely surprised. Then he shrugged. "In that case, I guess we'll just have to make this one my plate, and the next will be yours."

"Good idea," Haley agreed. With a determined effort, she managed to moderate the portions somewhat, this time around.

Carrying their food, they joined some friends who had spread out on the grass, grouped predictably around the ice-filled metal tub that held the keg of beer.

"Nice decor," Haley commented, patting the silver barrel as Dan topped off several mugs and passed them around. "I always said T. J. had a flair for coming up with just the right centerpiece."

"Did I hear someone mention my name?" T. J. inquired, setting down her plate on the grass and sitting down beside them.

"Yes, you did," Dan admitted. "But now that you're here, I guess we'll all have to stop talking about you. Gang?" he called teasingly, looking around the circle. "No more cracks about T. J. now, okay?"

"Okay!" they answered as one, grinning conspiratorially.

"What fun are you?" T. J. grumbled good-naturedly, biting into her hamburger. "How else am I supposed to find out what people are saying behind my back?"

"Try a hidden tape recorder," Haley suggested lightly. She

picked up a plastic fork and began to eat, too. "Take my word for it; it works every time."

Almost two hours passed before she saw Adam again. Between talking and drinking and dancing, Haley soon found that she lost track of the time. Although she wondered occasionally where Adam could have gotten himself off to, she ceased to worry over his whereabouts. He was a big boy now, she decided irritably. He could take care of himself. And if he didn't care enough to come and seek her out, well, then, that was his problem!

When she did find him again, it happened quite by accident.

Ducking into the house for a quick trip to the ladies' room, Haley took a short cut through the kitchen on the return trip. There, to her surprise, she discovered Adam, who was leaning over to peer intently into the well-stocked refrigerator while a tall, beautiful blonde of the Playmate-of-the-Month variety draped herself over his body from the side.

"Ahem," Haley said loudly, stopping in the middle of the room. No wonder he'd been so unavailable. Now that she knew who had been occupying his time, she could see the reason why! If he thought she was going to turn tail and slink away like a thief in the night, then he was dead wrong! Just who did he think he was, anyway?

Slowly, Adam straightened, then turned to face her. The refrigerator door swung shut behind him with a firm thump, and the blonde took the opportunity to solidify her position, winding one arm over his shoulder and the other about his waist as she continued to stand beside him. The look she gave Haley was frankly triumphant.

"Looking for something?" Haley inquired sweetly. Like a fat lip, she added silently to herself.

"Ice water," said Adam, his voice clipped, curt.

"Top shelf," Haley replied, equally terse.

Shouldering him and his appendage aside, she pulled open the door, yanked out the pitcher of ice water and sloshed some into a glass. She handed it to Adam, who immediately passed it over to the blonde.

"Haley Morgan," he said, nodding first in one direction, then the other. "Melanie Dubois."

"Pleased to meet you," Haley said automatically, then frowned. Lord, she thought, what a stupid thing to say when obviously nothing could be farther from the truth!

"I haven't seen you in quite a while," Adam commented, gazing at her thoughtfully. "Are you having a good time?"

"Just peachy," Haley snapped. She glared at the blonde, who continued to lean on Adam as though her life depended on it. "How about you?"

Adam shrugged, and Haley's eyes narrowed further.

"I think we'd better talk," he said suddenly. Gently disengaging himself from the blonde, he leaned her against the counter, then grasped Haley's arm and pulled her across the room to a door that led off into the den. "If you'll excuse us, Melanie?"

"Of course," the woman simpered, the first words she'd managed thus far.

Pulling her into the den, Adam pushed the door shut behind them, then stood before it to bar her exit.

"She's very pretty," Haley commented scathingly. Damn but she was jealous! Even knowing how Adam felt about that childish emotion, she still couldn't help her response. If Melanie had still been within reach, she would have been delighted to scratch the other woman's eyes out. "Pity she can't talk."

Adam's features hardened angrily.

"But then," she added caustically, "maybe with what you had in mind, talking wasn't going to be necessary."

Good God, who was this person inhabiting her body, saying these awful things? Haley wondered, struggling to bring her temper under control. Talk about playing with fire! Adam would be furious, but she couldn't seem to stop. All she had to do was open her mouth and the vitriolic words kept popping out!

"Haley, what's the matter with you?"

"Dammit!" she swore, giving her frustration free rein. "I've been missing you all evening, wondering where you were. And now I find out that all the time you've been with that—that—"

"Melanie," Adam supplied tersely.

"Yes, Melanie!" Haley snapped.

"You can't have been too concerned," Adam growled. "Every time I've seen you, you were out on the dance floor looking as though you were having the time of your life!"

"I wasn't," Haley insisted. "I was looking for you."

"Where?" Adam asked skeptically. "Through Phillips' pockets? Because the way the two of you were dancing together, you damn near could have been!"

"You're a fine one to talk. If Melanie had been standing any closer, she'd have been behind you!"

"She was feeling faint," said Adam. Pacing across the room, he reached up and thrust back his hair impatiently with one hand. "Although why I should have to explain myself to you, of all people—"

At that, Haley reacted as though she had been slapped. Her eyes filled with tears, which she blinked rapidly away as she swung around and fumbled for the doorknob. "You're right!" she cried defiantly. "You don't have to explain anything to me, Adam Burke. Not now and not ever!"

Throwing open the door, she dashed out through the kitchen. Blindly, she ran past Melanie, who was still waiting where Adam had left her, and out the back door. She'd gone no more than a few yards when someone grabbed her arm and swung her out onto the patio dance floor. Numb with pain, Haley followed mindlessly, uncaring of where she went or with whom.

It was a full fifteen minutes before she came to her senses, and by that time she was feeling pretty foolish. What on earth had ever possessed her to come down on Adam that way? She'd known all along that he didn't believe in jealousy, that he thought it was a destructive emotion. And if that night's experience was anything to go by, she could only agree that he was right. After all, look how close she had come to letting it destroy the wonderful new relationship that was blossoming between them! Despite Melanie's blonde, buxom assets, she should never have let herself jump to conclusions that way. She knew Adam better than that—much better—and certainly well enough to feel more trust in him than she had displayed thus far that night!

Without a backward glance toward the noisy party, Haley hurried inside, hoping Adam might still be there and that he would accept her apology. Instead, in the kitchen, she found only T. J., who was standing at the counter arranging several more platters of chopped vegetables and dip.

"Oh, good, I'm glad you're here. I have a message for you," said T. J., looking up as Haley entered the room. She paused and popped a raw carrot into her mouth and munched on it noisily. "You met Melanie, didn't you?"

Haley nodded, taking one of the platters from T. J.'s outstretched hand.

"She wasn't feeling too well and needed a ride home. Apparently, she came with a whole group of people and didn't have her own car, so Adam offered to drive her." Oblivious to the clouds that had gathered suddenly over Haley's features, T. J. rambled on. "She lives in North Stamford, and he said to tell you that he'd be back as soon as he could, and you're to wait here."

"Got it," Haley replied listlessly, feeling all at once as though all the wind had been knocked out of her body.

So much for reconciliation, she thought crossly. Of all the times for Adam to decide to play Good Samaritan! Summoning a reluctant smile, she followed T. J. out the door. Oh, well, there was nothing she could do about it now. Besides, Stamford wasn't that far away. Adam would probably be back in no time. . . .

The next two hours were quite possibly the longest Haley had ever spent. When midnight came and went and still Adam had not returned, she knew she was not going to wait any longer. Bypassing Jeff's offer of a ride, she managed instead to wedge herself into a carful of noisy revelers, who were only too glad to make the small detour necessary to drop her outside her door.

Once there, however, Haley was at a loss. Too edgy to sleep, she settled instead for a long, hot shower that soothed her jangled nerves but did nothing to ease the raw, burning ache that felt as though it were eating through her body from the inside out.

So Melanie was feeling faint, was she? Haley thought angrily, pacing back and forth across her small living room. That was a likely story! She'd seen the predatory way the blonde had staked out Adam for her own. And it wasn't as if he'd been protesting, either! In fact, the two of them had been all but embracing right before her eyes! She had every right to be jealous after witnessing a scene like that. And if Adam Burke didn't believe in the emotion, then that was his tough luck!

Abruptly, Haley stopped short, hands balling into fists at her sides as she remembered something else Adam had said that long-ago evening on the dance floor. That the only good reason for two people to be together was because that's where they both wanted to be—that there was no use in trying to hang onto a relationship that had already run its course. Is that what had happened to them? she wondered. Now that the book was completed, was the romance that was tied to it so irrevocably over as well?

Slumping down onto the sofa, her shoulders sagging in defeat, Haley sighed. If Adam had meant to let her know that he wanted his freedom back, he certainly couldn't have picked a more graphic way of getting the message across. And if that's what he wanted, then he could have it! She had no intention of binding herself to him like a ball and chain.

She was so deep in thought that it was a moment before Haley realized that the loud, jangling noise that roused her from her reverie belonged to the telephone. "What in the world?" she muttered irritably, leaping up off the couch and dashing into the bedroom to snatch up the receiver. Stretched out crosswise on the bed, she fitted the phone to her ear.

It was Adam.

"I had a flat tire," he announced without preamble. His voice, stretching across the distance separating them, sounded incredibly tired.

But by now Haley was tired as well. Emotionally and spiritually depleted, she was in no mood to listen to any excuses. What he had done was bad enough—thoughtless and rude and inconsiderate. She'd be damned if he was going to get away with thinking that one belated phone call could smooth everything over.

"Like hell you did," she replied scathingly. What kind of a fool did he take her for, anyway? "You've had three hours to think about it, Adam. Are you sure you couldn't have come up with a better excuse than that?"

"It's no excuse," Adam asserted forcibly. "It's the truth."

Sighing deeply, Haley said nothing at all.

"Haley, are you there?"

"Yes, Adam," she said slowly, defeat and disillusion eating into her like a knife. At least he might have had the decency to tell her the truth!

"What are you thinking?" he demanded.

"Don't lie to me, Adam," Haley said wearily. All at once, she felt a thousand years old, light years away from the happy young woman who had accompanied him to the party earlier that evening. "It doesn't take three hours to change a flat tire; even I know that. If you wanted to spend some time with Melanie, why didn't you just say so—"

"Melanie be damned!" Adam roared. Wincing, Haley held the receiver away from her ear. "Would you listen to me, Haley? You're the only woman I want—"

"Say what you like, Adam," Haley broke in. Knowing that he had to be lying about the flat tire, how could she believe anything that he might say? "It's all just so many words. You're very good with them."

"I should be. I'm a writer, remember?" Adam snapped, and she flinched at the heavy overlay of mockery in his tone.

Enough! Haley thought angrily. She'd heard all she wanted to. They were only talking in circles, anyway. "Good night, Adam," she said curtly.

"Good night?" he repeated incredulously. "Haley, what the hell—!"

Drawing a deep, unsteady breath, she lifted the receiver away from her ear and dropped it into the cradle. It was still rocking back and forth when the first hot, burning tears began to fall.

10

By the next morning, Haley had come to several conclusions, none of them pleasant. After a long, sleepless night, spent tossing and turning uselessly in bed, she had finally risen just before dawn, filled with the hopeless acceptance of what she had to do.

This time things would be different, she told herself firmly. She'd learned from her past mistakes and would not repeat them. Never again would she sacrifice everything for which she had worked so hard on account of a love affair gone wrong. Just because that one aspect of the relationship had soured didn't mean that she and Adam couldn't continue to work together as they had in the past. It was simply a matter of taking them both back to where they'd been before the romance entered their lives and turned them upside down.

Even determined as she was, however, Haley knew it would be no easy task. How naive she had been to think that she could handle deepening her relationship with Adam! If only she had read the signs, she'd have known right from the start that he was a man who could capture not only her mind and her body but her heart and her soul as well, and that once his, she would never again be the same.

Now, with the thought of his tenderness, his caring, his lovemaking, still fresh in her mind, the notion of giving Adam up seemed an impossibility, an insurmountable task. And yet she knew it had to be done.

She had to get away, Haley decided, knowing, even as she did so, that running was the coward's way out. Still, she felt a pressing need to escape, to flee, to put real physical distance between them. She needed time to think and try to put things in perspective, and she couldn't do it there. Her leaving would give them both an opportunity to cool off and calm down. But most important, it would give their relationship a chance to rest and, hopefully, to return to normal so that they would be able to work together once more.

In that regard, Haley was determined to be totally realistic. If she and Adam could not be lovers, then they would be friends and partners. She would settle for what she could get and make it enough. That she was deeply in love with him was just something she would have to learn to live with—live with and try to conceal for the sake of their working relationship.

It took Haley half an hour to shower and dress and less time than that to stuff the few items she would need at her parents' beach house into a suitcase. Lugging the bag into the next room, she set it down beside the door, then paused, frowning uncertainly.

She couldn't just vanish, Haley realized. Adam was sure to wonder where she had gotten to. And yet she couldn't call him, either. Aside from the obvious problem that it was only six o'clock in the morning, she knew that her nerves were shot, her emotions still too raw and close to the surface, for her to chance speaking to Adam right now. In fact, Haley thought sadly, the way she was feeling, she wouldn't be at all surprised to find herself breaking down into tears and confessing her undying love. All things considered, that wouldn't do at all.

With a deep, heartfelt sigh, she walked across the living room into the alcove where the two typewriters sat waiting. A feeling of inevitability directed her actions as Haley pulled out the chair and sat down behind her Smith-Corona.

Two hours later, the Rabbit was still parked in the garage, the suitcase was still waiting by the door, and Haley was still seated behind the typewriter, her features now screwed into an ominous scowl.

This was madness! she thought, drumming her fingers on the table top irritably. Sheer and utter insanity to think that she would ever be able to compose a note informing the man she loved that their relationship was over and his freedom restored. If she had any sense at all, she'd have given up on the attempt an hour earlier!

The first inkling Haley had that she had run out of time was the distinctive sound of the Zee's powerful motor as the car glided up her driveway. "Damn!" she swore vehemently. Snatching the latest sheet of paper out of the typewriter, she crumpled it up in her hand and tossed it over her shoulder to join the dozens of others already scattered about her chair. "That still isn't right!"

She heard the front door open but didn't look up. Instead, very deliberately, Haley concentrated on picking up another piece of paper and rolling it through the machine. The soft beat of Adam's footsteps across the hardwood floor attested to the fact that he was coming closer, but still, perversely, she ignored him. What was there to say, anyway?

"Oh, my God," Adam whispered softly, and Haley paused, finally daring to meet his gaze.

The expression she saw on his face was something akin to pain, and her breath caught in her throat as Adam's eyes swept around the room, taking in the mute evidence of the suitcase waiting by the door, her tired, red-rimmed eyes and the rejected balls of wadded up paper that surrounded her. Bending low, he swept one of the notes up off the floor, uncrumpled it and read the message.

"Good Lord, woman," he muttered under his breath incredulously, "You're writing me a 'Dear John' letter." Slowly, he looked around at the other papers scattered about the floor and frowned. "How many drafts have you done so far?"

Whatever response Haley had expected, that was certainly

not it! "Fourteen," she admitted, feeling distinctly uncomfortable beneath the penetrating glare of his scrutiny. "I couldn't seem to get the words right."

"So I can see," said Adam, scanning the note he was holding. "This is rubbish."

At that, Haley forgot her reticence. Automatically, she leaped to defend her work. "It may not have been my best effort," she declared, more than a little affronted by his tone, "but it wasn't *that* bad."

"It's not the style that's bothering me," Adam growled. "It's the content." Walking over to the table, he smoothed out the sheet of paper on its glass top, then leaned down to read it aloud. "What does this say?" he muttered. " 'I hope we can still be friends'?"

Slowly, Haley nodded.

Adam shook his head disparagingly. "That sounds like a line out of a bad movie."

"I know," she admitted, totally bewildered by his whole attitude but deciding to play along. "That must be one of the earlier drafts you're looking at." Leaning up in her chair, she stretched over the table so that she could see the paper, then nodded, confirming her guess. "Now that line reads, "I will always think of you as my dearest friend, and I hope you feel the same way about me."

"Hmmm," Adam said thoughtfully. "That's better, but there's still something missing."

"What?" asked Haley, looking up at him in surprise. Surely he wasn't planning to collaborate on his own "Dear John" letter, was he?

"There's no passion in your writing, no fire, no emotion! You've let it go flat."

"Big deal!" Haley scoffed, feeling perilously close to a hysterical giggle. If only he knew how hard she had worked to accomplish just that! "We can't all be great romantics. You're my partner. You should know better than anybody what sort of work I'm capable of."

"You're right," he murmured. "I do. And that's exactly why I refuse to let you go!"

Abruptly, Adam straightened. Grasping her shoulders, he pulled her up out of the chair and into his arms, and Haley followed his lead joyously, recklessly, uncaring of the fact that one more taste of paradise would make it that much harder to leave behind. For now she knew only that Adam wanted her, and she would not, could not, turn him away.

He covered her mouth with his, and Haley rose to meet him with a need that matched his own. Then, suddenly, the tempo changed. Taking his time, Adam teased her lips apart with his tongue, kissing her tenderly, longingly, even she thought somewhere in the deep inner reaches of her mind, lovingly.

No! Haley denied wildly. She couldn't allow herself to fall into that trap again. He'd just said it himself, after all—it was because he valued her work that he couldn't let her go.

Feeling suddenly, utterly vulnerable, Haley sighed deeply, a painful, aching sound that caused Adam to finally end the kiss, though the arms that curved possessively around her shoulders did not relinquish their hold.

"You don't have to worry," she said raggedly. "I was planning on coming back in a couple of weeks. We'll still be able to work together as usual." Haley knew she was babbling but was quite unable to stop. "Who knows, maybe by that time we'll have come up with a good idea for the next book."

"I couldn't care less about the next book. Don't you know that by now?" Adam growled. "That's not what's important to me—you are." His hand traveled up the smooth column of her throat until his fingers cupped her chin. Gently, he tilted her face up to his. "I love you, Haley Morgan. And if you are seriously entertaining any notions about running away from me, you'd better forget them right now, because if you do, I will follow you to the ends of the earth!" He paused and looked down at her solemnly. "Am I making myself clear?"

"Very," Haley replied, smiling tremulously.

Suddenly words seemed inadequate to convey the world of

glorious possibility that had just opened up to her. He loved her! The words rang through her mind like a clarion call, bringing with them a tide of elation so strong that her smile widened into an idiotic grin. Adam Burke loved her!

Then, quite without warning, a small seed of irritation began to grow. Damn the man, anyway! thought Haley. How dare he wait until the eleventh hour to get around to making his feelings known? My God, if she had been used to writing solo, she'd have been long since gone, and then where would he have been?

"You took your own sweet time letting me know," she grumbled unreasonably.

"I told you once before that I didn't want to rush you," Adam said softly. "You said yourself you were afraid that we were identifying too closely with our characters, and I agreed. Now that the book is finished, I'd planned to give you some time to get Allegra out of your system so that we could start fresh and go from there. The last thing I expected you to do was try and run away."

Remembering the anguished hours she'd just spent, Haley sighed. "Why didn't you tell me this last night?"

"I tried to call," Adam pointed out.

"That was hours ago."

"I know." Adam frowned. "I've been up, counting them."

Dark eyes open wide, Haley gazed up at him. "You, too?"

Adam nodded. "I wanted to come over here right away. In fact, I almost did. But after the way our phone conversation had gone, I was afraid you'd slam the door in my face. I spent the rest of the night hoping maybe a good night's sleep would improve your disposition."

Haley shook her head sadly. "I was a little quick with you," she admitted. Drawing her lower lip into her mouth, she chewed on it thoughtfully. "Did you really have a flat tire?"

"Two, actually," Adam confirmed. "It turned out that the spare was flat as well. And at that hour of the night, I had to walk almost three miles before I could find an open gas station."

"Poor Adam," Haley murmured. Slipping her fingers inside the open throat of his shirt, she let them nestle in the soft hair she found there. "And what was Melanie doing all this time?" she asked casually.

Grinning, Adam shrugged. "I don't know, and I don't care. Fortunately, this all happened on the way *back* to the party. By that time, I'd had enough of Miss Dubois to last me a lifetime!"

"Really?" Haley said, trying hard not to look too interested. "From what I could see, the two of you seemed to be getting along quite well."

Stroking her hair gently with his hand, Adam gazed down into her eyes. "What you saw didn't mean a thing," he said seriously. "She may have hoped that it did, and I'll admit I wasn't exactly going out of my way to discourage her, but to tell the truth, it was all self-defense on my part. Outside, I'd been going crazy watching you captivate nearly every man at that party. I needed desperately to get away, and when Melanie announced that she wasn't feeling well and asked if I would find her something cold to drink, it seemed like the perfect excuse."

"Nearly every man at the party . . . ?" Haley repeated slowly, incredulously. What on earth was he talking about? His perception was far from the truth, yet there was only one reason she could think of to explain his feelings. "Adam?" she said softly. "Were you jealous?"

It was a moment before he answered, a moment in which his features hardened in self-deprecation. "I know," he said, his voice suddenly harsh. "It's a laugh, isn't it? All those noble speeches I made about jealousy having no place in a good relationship, and then suddenly for the first time in my life, I was putting those beliefs to the test and finding out just how wrong they were. Imagine how I felt when I took one look at you dancing in that octopus's arms and realized that I wanted to wring his neck with my bare hands!"

"But you smiled," Haley sputtered in confusion. "You even waved."

Adam pursed his lips ruefully. "You didn't see my other

hand—it was clenched into a fish at my side. That's when I knew that if I didn't get my mind off you soon, I was going to do something we'd both regret."

"So you found Melanie," Haley said slowly, nodding to herself.

"Actually," Adam corrected her, "Melanie found me. I'd been talking to some people whose names I couldn't keep straight about topics I cared nothing about when she draped herself over my shoulder and asked if I knew my way around the house."

Haley arched one eyebrow upward. "Do you mean to say that that poor, sweet thing couldn't manage to find the kitchen all on her own?"

Adam grinned sheepishly. "Like I said, I was desperate. Then, by some miracle, I managed to get you away, all to myself, and the next thing I knew, we were fighting."

"And the next thing *I* knew," said Haley, "you were gone. I came right back looking for you, only to be told that you'd left with Melanie."

"If only I'd known." Adam groaned. "I guess I wasn't thinking straight, but at the time, I had it all figured out in my mind that you couldn't wait to get back to the party. All I knew was that the moment I stepped away from the door, you bolted through it!"

"So you drove Melanie home."

Adam shrugged. "Somebody had to. Besides, it seemed like we both needed a chance to cool off."

"Somebody had to?" Haley repeated, biting back a smile. "If you ask me, Melanie looked about as sick as a blue-ribbon, corn-fed heifer."

At that, Adam looked faintly embarrassed. "It turned out she wasn't anywhere near as faint as she'd pretended to be. In fact, by the time I got her home, she seemed to have made a rather miraculous recovery. She even went so far as to suggest that I come inside and tuck her into bed."

"And did you?" Haley asked interestedly.

"You know the answer to that," Adam growled.

"Do I?"

Adam paused to think. "Actually," he admitted, "you don't know all of it." Taking her hand in his, he led her over to the couch. He sat down on the plump cushions, then pulled her down onto his lap, his expression earnest and intent. "I told Melanie that I couldn't possibly come inside because I was engaged to a woman I loved far too much to ever dream of hurting like that."

Haley had been wriggling provocatively across Adam's knees, settling herself comfortably on his lap, but now she shot bolt upright onto her feet. *"You told her what?"*

Slowly, carefully, Adam pulled her back down into place, then repeated his words. Raising the hand that he held, he buried his lips in her palm, and Haley let her fingers curl around to cup the sides of his jaw. "I told her I was going to be married. Is it true, kid?"

"I don't know," she whispered, her face reflecting the shock she felt. Predictably, the first words that popped into her head popped out of her mouth as well. "Is this a proposal?"

The look Adam gave her was tinged with exasperation. "Can't you tell?"

Suddenly, Haley felt more light-hearted than she had in weeks. She wanted to laugh and cry all at the same time. Instead, she settled for shaking her head teasingly. "Rex got down on one knee for his."

"Rex," Adam said succinctly, "was a sap."

"Oh, I don't know," Haley commented. "There is something to be said for the good old-fashioned approach. After all, it worked on Allegra."

Adam, however, was in no mood to be teased. Looking down at her, he scowled ominously. "If you don't answer me soon, you might find yourself the victim of the frustrated he-man approach!"

Nodding to herself thoughtfully, Haley slid her hands slowly up Adam's arms, then across his shoulders until they met in the middle on the front placket of his shirt. Leisurely, she pulled the buttons free of their holes one by one, exposing a strip of warm, hair-covered flesh. Then, using just the tip of one finger, she traced a winding trail downward, delighting in the shudder that rippled suddenly through Adam's body.

"Does this mean that it's time for another hands-on experience?" she drawled.

"Definitely," Adam agreed with a wolfish grin. Abruptly, his hand snaked out to capture hers and pull it to a halt. "But first, there's still one small bit of business to be dealt with." Gazing deeply into her eyes, he asked, "Will you marry me, kid?"

Haley smiled radiantly. "I love you, Adam, more than anything else in the whole world. And I thought you'd never ask." She reached out to draw him to her, but still Adam held her away.

"Is that a yes or a no?" he demanded.

"That's yes, boss," Haley whispered, and suddenly the restraints were gone.

"That's what I like," Adam murmured, his voice husky with male satisfaction, "a woman who knows her place."

"Um hm," Haley nodded agreeably. She leaned her weight into him, and he fell back against the cushions. Then, lying stretched out full-length over him, she propped her hands on his chest and smiled downward complacently. "On top."

Unexpectedly, Adam's arms came out to circle her body, holding her close while he executed a quick flip. "And sometimes," he drawled, "on the bottom."

Haley grinned. "It's a point I'll look forward to negotiating."

Above her, Adam nodded. "I'm sure we'll be able to reach some sort of agreement."

"Many, I should think," Haley agreed solemnly.

Threading her fingers through his thick brown hair, she drew Adam's head down to her own, joining them in a kiss that was gentle, tender, yet devastating in its intensity—a reaffirmation of the commitment they now shared.

When at last he lifted his head and paused for breath, Haley sighed contentedly. There was no need to hurry now. They had the rest of their lives to savor the passion that flowed between them. "You know," she said dreamily, "I guess we have Rex and Allegra to thank for finally bringing us together."

"Rex and Allegra, nothing!" Adam growled, and Haley blinked several times, startled by his vehemence. Then, seeing that she still didn't understand, he added, "Whose idea was it to write a romance in the first place?"

Taken totally by surprise, Haley's mouth dropped open, then snapped shut. "Do you mean to tell me that you planned all this?" she asked incredulously.

Adam nodded, clearly satisfied with himself. "I had to do something. You'd imposed so many restrictions on our relationship, I was beginning to go quietly crazy. Our friendship was fine, but I was sure that if you'd only let it happen, we could have much, much more."

"So you decided to seduce me with your flowing rhetoric, is that it?"

Much to Haley's surprise, Adam suddenly looked quite put out. "Damn!" he swore softly. "And all this time I thought it was my sexy body you couldn't resist!"

"There is that, too," Haley said happily, snuggling closer. Then she grinned. "Now that I know what you were up to, I have to admit *Passionate Strangers* made a very effective smokescreen. But after all that work we put into it, do you think it will ever be published?"

Smiling down at her, Adam shrugged. "I don't care," he murmured. "I've got everything I wanted."

"So have I," Haley agreed, rising to meet his lips with her own. "So have I."

Silhouette Desire

Now Available

Fabulous Beast by Stephanie James

Before, Tabitha had only studied the elusive
beasts of legend. Then she rescued Dev Colter
from danger on a remote island and
found that she had awakened a
slumbering dragon

Political Passions by Suzanne Michelle

Newly-elected mayor Wallis Carmichael was
furious to discover that sensual Sam Davenport
was really a Pulitzer Prize-winning journalist.
Politics and journalism don't mix—and now
she had to find out if he was just another
reporter out for a story.

Madison Avenue Marriage
by Cassandra Bishop

Famous mystery writer Lily Lansden needed a
"husband" for her winery commercial and
Trent Daily fitted the bill. But when the
game of pretend turned into real love could
Lily give up her Madison Avenue marriage?

Silhouette Desire

Now Available

Between the Covers by Laurien Blair

Everything changed between co-authors Adam
and Haley when they began writing their ninth
book together—a romance. Were they only
playing out a story or were they friends now
unleashing desires restrained for too long?

To Touch the Fire by Shirley Larson

Raine had loved Jade since she was sixteen—
but he was her sister's husband. Now her
sister had left him—would his bitterness
and her guilt over the past threaten
their awakening passions?

**On Love's Own Terms
by Cathlyn McCoy**

Luke Ford had been out of Bonnie's life for
seven years. But now her devastating husband
wanted a second chance, and Bonnie's common
sense was betrayed by a passion that
still burned.

Silhouette Desire

Coming Next Month

Love And Old Lace by Nicole Monet

Burned once, Virginia had decided to swear off romance and settle for a sensible, chaste existence—but seductive Lucas Freeman stormed her defences and neither her body nor her heart could resist.

Wilderness Passion by Lindsay McKenna

Libby wanted to be ready for anything when she met her unwilling partner on the environmental expedition. But nothing prepared her for Don Wagner, and the mountain trek suddenly became a journey into a world of desire.

Table For Two by Josephine Charlton

Hadley and Lucas had shared a youthful love. Now, when Hadley had landed in his embrace once more, history repeated itself and left them both determined that this time they would not have to say goodbye.

Silhouette Desire

Coming Next Month

The Fires Within by Aimee Martel

As a female firefighter, Isabel was
determined to be "one of the boys"—but no
one made her feel more a woman than Lt. Mark
Grady. Passion blazed between them, but
could they be lovers *and* co-workers?

Tide's End by Erin Ross

Chemical engineer on an offshore oil rig,
Holly had vowed never to engage in a
"platform romance". Kirk's touch could
make her forget her promises, but would his
dangerous job as a diver keep them apart?

Lady Be Bad by Elaine Raco Chase

Though Noah had broken her heart six years
before, Mariayna still loved him. Now she
would attend his wedding with only one aim
in mind—she would break all the rules
to have him back again.

THE MORE SENSUAL
PROVOCATIVE ROMANCE

95p each

115 □ GAMBLER'S
WOMAN
Stephanie James

116 □ CONTROLLING
INTEREST
Janet Joyce

117 □ THIS BRIEF
INTERLUDE
Nora Powers

118 □ OUT OF
BOUNDS
Angel Milan

119 □ NIGHT WITH
A STRANGER
Nancy John

120 □ RECAPTURE
THE LOVE
Rita Clay

121 □ LATE RISING
MOON
Dixie Browning

122 □ WITHOUT
REGRETS
Brenda Trent

123 □ GYPSY
ENCHANTMENT
Laurie Paige

124 □ COLOUR MY
DREAMS
Edith St. George

125 □ PASSIONATE
AWAKENING
Gina Caimi

126 □ LEAVE ME
NEVER
Suzanne Carey

127 □ FABULOUS
BEAST
Stephanie James

128 □ POLITICAL
PASSIONS
Suzanne Michelle

129 □ MADISON
AVENUE
MARRIAGE
Cassandra Bishop

130 □ BETWEEN THE
COVERS
Laurien Blair

131 □ TO TOUCH
THE FIRE
Shirley Larson

132 □ ON LOVE'S
OWN TERMS
Cathlyn McCoy

All these books are available at your local bookshop or newsagent, o
can be ordered direct from the publisher. Just tick the titles you want an
fill in the form below.
Prices and availability subject to change without notice.

SILHOUETTE BOOKS, P.O. Box 11, Falmouth, Cornwall.

Please send cheque or postal order, and allow the following for postag
and packing:

U.K. – 50p for one book, plus 20p for the second book, and 14p fo
each additional book ordered up to a £1.63 maximum.

B.F.P.O. and EIRE – 50p for the first book, plus 20p for the secon
book, and 14p per copy for the next 7 books, 8p per book thereafter

OTHER OVERSEAS CUSTOMERS – 75p for the first book, plu
21p per copy for each additional book.

Name ....

Address ....

....